RISING SUN OVER THE DEVIL'S NEST

BY SIRIUS

Curious Corvid
PUBLISHING

For Ellis,

There is nothing I can say.

A total eclipse of the heart.

For Janus,

Even if you are part of the FBI.

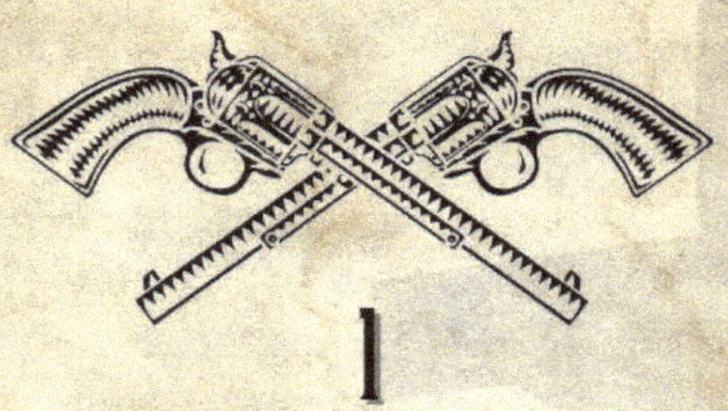

1

Through his peephole, Abraham could see the vampire. The warped fisheye lens skewed his visitor's proportions and made it easy to get distracted by gleaming ivory fangs and the quiet threat of busy, thin fingers trailing over the rotted screen door. He had not heard anyone walk up, and probably would not have gone to the door if his dog had not started whining and scratching at the knob. Quincey still had a nose for the preternatural despite the years that were piling onto his gray, drooping face.

The visitor's long nails continued to pick at the holes in the torn screen. Abraham let go of a deep sigh he had been holding and looked down at his bloodhound.

"What do you think?" He asked. His dog did not respond. Quincey had already laid back down and clearly considered his job done. He just looked up at his master with large, doleful black eyes half-buried under a sagging brow.

"Oh, come now, Mr. Helsing," the voice from outside carried an affected pompous accent that had not been displaced despite centuries of being knocked in the head. "How long are we going to continue this dance before we can speak as gentlemen?"

"Gentlemen?" Abraham scoffed out loud and turned the bent knob that barely served to keep his door closed. "I declare, Mr. Dracula, your definition of what makes a *gentleman* is as loose as a…" he did not finish his sentence. It trailed off into the hot Southern night and took his tongue with it in the face of the vampire that he had not encountered in well over a decade.

Dracula had been dead for so long that his skin was the color of gnarled lavender left to dry out in a summer wreathe. Underneath the foggy porch light, he looked downright plum-colored, and his maroon eyes glistened from underneath his dark, sweeping brows like twin cuts of fresh meat. He was dressed in all the finery from his centuries-old trunks, moth-eaten brocade and thinning velvet that weighed his sleight frame down and threatened to wrap around his heeled boots.

Prior to meeting Dracula, Abraham had never seen a creature dead or alive that quite matched that shade of the grave. He had choked plenty of monsters until they were blue in the face and pounded a number of stakes through an even greater number of hearts. Busting through a few veins was usually enough to turn their skin a nice, mottled shade of purple and red. But this one was paler, long dead as opposed to a new corpse – with a shock of cobalt hair and a white stripe running down the front bang as if death had struck him with the ferocity of a lightning bolt.

Dracula smiled and bared all his teeth.

"You are looking old," the vampire said.

"I feel older than I look," Abraham placed his hand against the dirty white wall and leaned close enough that the screen began to blur in his vision. "What do you want?"

"Down straight to business, are we?" The vampire combed his fingers coyly through his hair. "That is not very Southern hospitality of you, Mr. Helsing."

Abraham's nostrils flared and he straightened up his posture. "My apologies, but it has been a long week. And I was not expecting any visitors."

"So I heard," Dracula said. "About your week, I mean. It must be dreadful. Almost a decade of nothing and suddenly here you are, at it again with every creature between here and Georgia knocking on your door, making you really sing for your supper."

"Is that why you are here?" Abraham asked. "To make me sing?"

"No, no, not I. If anything, I am in a bit of a bind, and I was hoping that I might collect on an old debt." The vampire tilted his head, and for a moment his blood-red eyes were all Abraham could see through the screen door mesh. "But if now is not convenient, please accept my apologies. I do not mean to trouble you."

"Well," Abraham took a defeated step back, "it really is not any trouble."

"Do not allow me to intrude," Dracula cooed, long black nails scratching at his throat in a distressed gesture. "It is so late for humans, I forget. And a man of your age is usually abed by what – nine o' clock?"

"Respectfully, sir, you are pushing it," Abraham snipped.

"Of course, of course," Dracula's hands fluttered, although his smile did not diminish. "Well, then, if it really is no intrusion…?"

"No trouble at all, as I said. Do come in, I insist." Abraham stepped aside and Dracula's smile widened. The screen door opened by itself, swinging wide on loose hinges. Dracula stepped over the threshold, and Quincey was on his feet again – teeth bared, hackles raised.

Abraham realized what he had done. "Goddammit," escaped under his breath. He turned on his heel and started towards his well-lit kitchen while Quincey read ahead of him. "Every goddamn time…!"

"Now, Mr. Helsing," Dracula spread his hands. "There is no need for you to believe that I have ill intentions towards you or your…mongrel."

"Keep talking," Abraham swept his foot out and knocked one of the kitchen chairs off its feet, catching it in time to flip it over and snap off one of the legs. "You have about three minutes before I turn this into something I can use."

"How many perfectly good chairs have you wasted that way, really?" Dracula glanced down at his nails, seemingly unbothered by the makeshift stake. "This does not have to be like last time."

"Last time, in Verona, I had a proper stake."

"And little good it did you then, eh?" Dracula cackled. He pulled up the part of his cape that had been dragging along the ground and wrapped it around his arm. "All right, you dear old man. I can let you take a swing at me for free. I suppose I deserve it, for interrupting your re-runs of *Bonanza.*"

"Do me *some* credit. That television does not even work." Abraham pulled a few stray pieces away from the broken chair leg until the jagged end was as clean as he could make it. "You are running out of time."

"Your television does not work, but your record player does." Dracula hopped off the table and started walking towards the living room. Abraham followed him, gripping the table leg hard enough that his nails pressed dents into the glaze. "What do you listen to when you are all alone at night, Mr. Helsing? What is this?" The vampire picked up an empty vinyl sleeve. "Does this feature any of those instruments you are so fond of? I forget what they are called. Banjos?"

"You are down to thirty seconds," Abraham growled.

Dracula pursed his lips and set the empty sleeve back down.

"Banjos, you know," the vampire said, "are very closely related to mandolins. If you listen to the more traditional Romanian folk music, you will find them very inspired. In fact, I think the cousinhood of the banjo and the mandolin serves as a delightful metaphor for you and I, and how very similar we are in our natures when you get down to the wire."

Abraham rubbed his face. He eyed the glass of cold whiskey that he had left sweating on the little table beside his armchair and had forgotten about completely until that moment. "I am starting to think that you just came here to try and kill me again."

"Nonsense, I do not play with my food." Dracula gave him a long look. "And I have had plenty of opportunity to feed on you before now. If I wanted you dead, you would be."

A seditious silence swallowed up the room. It was a special talent that the count had. He was, in all ways, disarming and ridiculous until the other shoe dropped. He could turn it all off in a flash, like a match on gunpowder, and the smoke that was left behind was all creature. It was very easy to forget he was not human, until it suddenly became impossible to ignore.

Abraham relaxed his shoulders. It was easier, more comfortable, when he could recognize what he was dealing with. He kept his grip on the table leg, but his heart was no longer racing at a hundred miles an hour. He knew the vampire had the ability to hear his blood rush in his ears as well as he could.

"You mentioned an old debt," Abraham prompted, and broke the silence.

"A *very* old debt," Dracula acknowledged. "Back when we first encountered one another. What do you remember about that evening?"

"More than I ought to. Way more than I would like," Abraham replied.

"We waltzed together in the moonlight, you and I." Dracula sighed. "You tried to stab me at every turn, and I caught you almost every time. We were entwined in one another's arms, locked in a deadly embrace with your pulse throbbing in your throat and your chest pressed so close to mine that I thought your heartbeat was my own, even though I had not felt my heart move in almost two centuries before that."

"So I recall," Abraham said, "so you have mentioned a dozen times since then."

"And I spared your life. Do you remember that?"

"Once again, you wouldn't let me forget."

"And it was not just because I thought you were a handsome devil," the vampire said. "Although you really were, you know. It was nothing to be wasted bleeding out on the stones of my estate. And I knew you would be of use to me, one day."

"That has not yet proven to be true," Abraham rotated a quarter turn and walked towards his chair, fairly confident that the vampire was not going to lunge and kill him within the next few minutes. He picked up his whiskey glass by the rim and raised it to his mouth. "There were just as many instances where I could have killed you, and I didn't. Is that not a debt paid? A life for a life?"

"Please, do be serious. My *life?*"

"It rolls off the tongue a fair bit easier than saying something like 'your godforsaken, abominable…"

"Please!"

"…And downright unholy existence'."

"Oh, now – draw it mild, you are getting me quite excited." The tips of Dracula's nails clattered against one another. "I am not trying to be unreasonable here, Abraham."

The use of his first name struck a nerve. Abraham almost spat out his whiskey, but instead he pushed it into his cheeks until it burned the torn tissue, and then he swallowed.

"Reasonable or not, it appears that I do not have a choice," he said at last. "So, how about you tell me what you came here for, Vladislav? We can address all the particulars at another time."

The vampire made a dissatisfied moue with his lips, but he moved on. "Do you remember the old bar that we used to frequent? It was called *Cyclone*, or something like that was in the name."

"*Cyclone Saloon.* I remember it. They closed it down, didn't they?"

"Yes, about half a decade ago, and long overdue. I am certain you remember that the place was a regular stye."

"Not that it mattered much to you, either way," Abraham grabbed the nearby whiskey bottle and refilled his glass. "You weren't exactly there for what they kept on tap."

"Ah," Dracula's smile was wistful. "You can say that blood filters it all the same."

Abraham knocked back half his glass. "So, they unplugged the neon sign and nailed up plywood over the windows. What does that have to do with me?"

"They closed it down for an infestation," Dracula drummed his fingertips against his sleeve.

"What, too many roaches in the deep fryer?"

"No," a smirk crawled over the vampire's mouth. "Too many bats."

Abraham paused, trying to muddle through the cryptic wording and put the pieces together. He was not as sharp as he used to be, and the whiskey did not help. "You have a notion?"

"I do," Dracula was practically preening. "You see, that old building sits right on the edge of what I consider to be *my territory*. And as you well know, I am dreadfully territorial. So, when bodies turn up rather messily slaughtered, where their throats have been ripped out and I have nothing to do with it…I get upset, and I am a fright when I am upset."

"If you could manage to circle back to the point of all this, sometime before the night is out, I would be grateful."

"Fine," the vampire's response was short and pettish. "A swarm of devils has taken up residence in the old bar. I hesitate to call them vampires, as I am fairly certain they have no intelligence or manners to speak of. However, with all that being said, there are far too many of them for me to try and command or eliminate. I cannot very well pull out many tricks from your hat, as what would be devastating to them would also be ruinous for me."

"Fire, holy water, the whole nine?" Abraham nodded. "At least I am finally starting to understand why you called upon me."

"It is a tremendous undertaking. I can think of no better man for the job."

Abraham could, easily. It was a big state. There were a dozen monster hunters within a few hours of the city who could make the trip on short notice.

They were all younger, too, which had its pros and cons. Still, he knew that it did not matter how many names on business cards he kept smashed together in his wallet. Dracula wanted *him*. And he had yet to see a day where the former aristocrat did not get his way.

"Is it your intention to have me drive down there tonight?" Abraham asked, resigning.

"There is still plenty of moonlight left," Dracula said. "And you are not getting any younger, are you?"

"No," that much was for certain. The years weighed down his shoulders like an old leather coat, and with each one that passed his arms felt a little heavier, he moved a little slower. He wasn't turning down jobs because he didn't need the money. He was turning them down because there were days when he couldn't get out of bed in the morning.

"I will go tomorrow during twilight hours," Abraham spoke again before Dracula could say anything else. The vampire was skimming through his record collection again, long black nails separating each album cover from their stack with ease. "Doesn't sound like something I want to drive into blind in the dead of night."

"Bonnie Tyler," Dracula did not even acknowledge what had been said to him. He pulled one record free from the very end of the stack, flashing a smile that almost appeared sentimental. "You really are a sap."

"Are you listening to me?" Abraham snapped, irritated. He closed the distance between them and snatched the record from the vampire's hands. "I said that I will see you tomorrow."

"Twilight hours are so unspeakably early," Dracula fussed.

"Goodnight, Vladislav," now that he had started saying it, he could not stop. "You are not staying here."

"I get the sense that you are still angry with me," Dracula flashed a smile as he pulled away. "You need to let some things go."

Abraham was about three seconds away from wrestling his crucifix free from his shirt collar. "You will find that I am under no obligation to do any such thing."

"After all that transpired between us? *Helsing,*" Dracula lowered his curling black lashes. "You would starve me with your neglect."

Abraham ground his teeth. "If you withered and died, I would not feel it."

"How awful," Dracula clucked his tongue. "And it is not even true. If you did not want to speak to me, you would not have even answered the door."

Abraham lapsed into silence. He pinched the gold crucifix underneath his shirt and rubbed it between his thumb and forefinger, grinding down against the ridges of the Christ figure. Dracula flashed his canines and winked, gathering up the edges of his cloak once again.

"I will see you tomorrow, Mr. Helsing," Dracula said. "Sleep well."

He was gone in column of acrid smoke. Abraham coughed into his arm and waved his hand around to try and get some of it to dissipate. The screen door banged against its frame, and from the kitchen, Quincey howled.

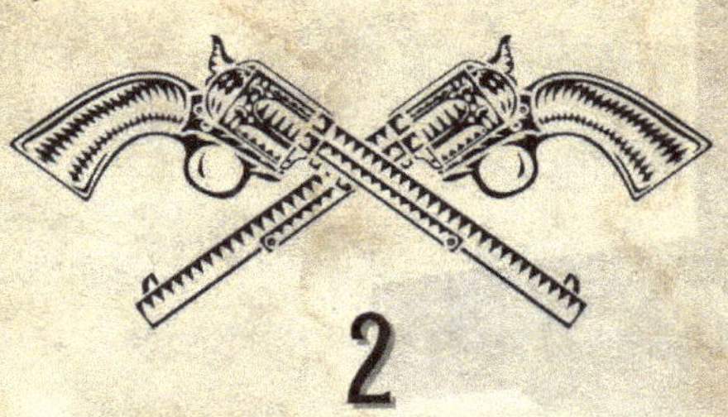

2

Dawn spit flame-red tongues across the sky and made the thin, wispy clouds look purple, like bruised and bloody welts. Abraham had not slept a bit. He had spent the majority of his night digging through an old cedar chest and dragging out some useless materials he swore he would never look through again. There were twelve water-stained journals recounting the last two decades and a bundle of photographs taken with a polaroid camera. There was a perfumed letter sealed in black wax and an old wooden crucifix that had broken in half, once, and he had glued it back together.

He burned everything except the crucifix and drank until he ran out of whiskey.

Now the world was muzzy, but everything was starting to feel familiar again. The only thing he couldn't really place his finger on was the exact moment he had decided to get into his truck and drive down to the old white church with blue cornflower fields. He had assumed it was abandoned, but apparently not.

The doors were always open, so he had no problem walking in. The dark wooden pews looked a little worn-down, but they were clean and showed signs of recent upkeep. He chose the furthest row in the back and sat down, regret churning along with the booze in his stomach.

There was a hymnal in the slot in front of him. It was new, green, with gold letters on the front that just said *Zion*. He picked it up and began to thumb through the pages. He wasn't sure why he did it, except he knew them all by heart. The pages still smelled like pages and the ink was crisp and dark in a way that kept him transfixed, despite knowing nothing about musical notes or bars or anything other than the tight, square words that were jammed into the middle and hyphenated in odd places.

"I have told you often enough," a voice broke him free of his reverie, "to take off your hat in church."

Abraham's heart jumped into his throat, and he looked up, his blood pumping so fast that it made his wrists hurt. He slammed the hymnal shut and stuck it back into the slot, reaching up to touch his head as if his hat was no longer going to be there.

"I'm just stopping by, reverend," he said. "Not here to bring any trouble."

"Trouble follows you, Abraham Van Helsing, like hellfire on the Devil's heels." The preacher sat down in the row ahead of him and turned to rest his arm along the back. The cavernous smile lines around his mouth did not make him look any friendlier than a bulldog. "But this is God's home, and you are always welcome here."

Abraham cleared his throat. He shifted in his seat, and all he could hear was the sound of leather groaning as he moved. "You've got a nice new sign out there," he said. "And nice new hymnals. Never seen these before."

"God is good," the preacher said, "all the time."

Abraham's regret was turning him nauseous.

"I guess I should have come sooner," he said, "but it didn't seem right."

"You are here now," the preacher told him. "That is all that matters. Tell me what is on your mind."

Abraham rubbed his face and dug his fingers into the corners of his eyes. It did nothing to chase out the headache that was starting to pile up behind them.

"I guess," he said, "you could say that I'm at a crossroads."

"You were at a crossroads many years ago, too," the preacher said. "What is it now?"

"I remember," Abraham gritted his teeth. "And I guess it is more or less the same. I'm not that boy anymore; there are a lot more bodies separating me from him."

"But some problems," the preacher hinted, "do not go away?"

"Some things just stick with you," Abraham said. "And it doesn't matter how hard you try to shake them off."

"And what's stuck to you, Abraham?"

He pushed his fingers so hard into his tear ducts that he saw stars. Abraham raised his head back up to force himself to stop.

"I think I am going to give it all up," he could not bring himself to say the deeper truth out loud. "You know, vampires, werewolves, ghouls… they will always be here, but I sure as hell won't be. I am getting old."

"Death's long shadow chases many men back to these doors," the preacher nodded his understanding.

"Death doesn't worry me," Abraham said. "Not like it should, I reckon." He dragged his nail down the edges of the hymnal in front of him, anything to avoid looking at the preacher's eyes. "But there is someone I've known for a while, and I think I'm ready to give him what he wants."

He had not brought himself there to admit that to anyone, not even to himself. Something about that place choked it out of him. It wrung a confession right out of his tongue and then just left it to writhe in the milquetoast hands of God's most pious bastard.

The preacher sighed. It was a heavy, relenting sound that Abraham recognized and resented.

"I know what you are going to say," Abraham spoke first.

"Do you?" The preacher asked.

"I do," Abraham sat up straight. "I've heard it all before. But it doesn't bother me anymore, reverend. This man, you don't know him, and he isn't perfect. Neither am I, at the end of the day. But he is all I've got, and I'm all he's got too. Being alone like that is a lot for two creatures to have in common." He wanted to say *people,* but it felt wrong. Dracula was a monster, and the waters were muddy enough.

"I think you misunderstand me," the preacher said. "I am not here to tell you about the things you are doing wrong." He reached across the row and gripped Abraham's upper arm. "You came here, to God's house, and I am going to tell you exactly what I have always said from the beginning. You are not alone. God is always with you. Lay your burdens down at his feet and accept him back into your life."

Abraham sucked in a breath, and it felt like barbed wire was squeezing the life out of his lungs. "You know," he growled, "I don't think I ever said that I stopped believing in God."

"No," the preacher said. His tone was nursery-soft and soothing. "But do you make room for God in your life, Abraham? Do you give Him the time of day? Do you walk with him, talk with him? Say your prayers at night?"

"Goddammit," Abraham tried to stand up. "I don't have any time for this."

The preacher's grip on his arm kept him from rising fully to his feet. Abraham sat back down hard, the teeth rattling in his head. The preacher held his gaze, and for a moment, Abraham considered slamming a knife through his jaw. It wouldn't have helped, but it would have made him feel better.

"Your time is running out," the preacher said. "You are the one who told me that."

"God loves me, but He's ashamed of me," Abraham retorted. "*You* are the one who told me that."

"He loves you just the way that you were made," the preacher's grip was cutting off the circulation in his arm. "It is your choice to live in sin, and that is what keeps you separated from the full of His light."

Abraham grabbed the preacher's wrist. He wanted to break it, but he just used his hold to make the old man release him instead. He stood, brushing off the arm of his coat as he did so.

"I have to go," he muttered. "I have someone to meet."

He turned without another word, and his boots struck resentfully against the floor as he showed himself out. If the reverend tried to say anything else, he did not hear it, and he wasn't interested.

3

His dusty engine sputtered as Abraham pulled into the abandoned parking lot, which at this point was nothing more than an unmarked square of brown earth covered in shriveled weeds. Not far from where he parked stood the remains of the *Cyclone Saloon*, and even from a distance, it was clear that the bar had seen way better days. Its neon sign had been robbed of its bulbs while every grimy window and door had been covered up with plywood and tape. A few raunchy flyers that promised enticing entertainment still clung in tatters to spots where not even the elements could pull off the glue.

Abraham ripped down one of the flyers and glanced at the sun-faded faces that had become all toothy grins and pixelated eyes staring back at him. Maybe all those girls were dead by now. He hoped not, but he couldn't know. He crumpled the paper up in his hand and released it to the breeze.

"It is just like you, I suppose, to be so unfashionably early." Dracula sniffed. Abraham had not heard him approach, but that wasn't so unusual. As long as the vampire was not within six feet of him without announcing his presence, he didn't give a damn.

"I was already about," Abraham replied. "And I didn't know when you would be here." He glanced over, taking in the large black umbrella that cast significant shade over the vampire's gloved fingers and the round, red-tinted sunglasses that shielded his eyes. "I guess you dressed for it."

"Yes, well, I do not wish for a repeat of our little moment in Lyon," Dracula said. "Although third degree burns are all well and good."

Abraham turned his eyes back towards the building. "You had a great deal of trouble sitting down, I do recall."

"It was a malevolent crime upon my *derrière,*" the count flashed a cheeky grin.

"Mm," Abraham grabbed the door handle and shook it. The door stuck fast, clanging angrily against the bolt. "You said that they have been nesting in here?"

"Yes, but you will not get in that way." Dracula looked at him. "You look as though you have not slept."

"I haven't," Abraham said shortly. He took a step back and started his making way around the side of the building, searching for an entry point that he could use. "I drove into town, ate some breakfast, went home and loaded up my truck. Came back out here."

"At least you will not be slicing off heads on an empty stomach." Dracula followed him, the tips of his dainty shoes skittering along the path of Abraham's long twilight shadow. "Although it is grisly work. I wonder if you will throw up."

"I haven't thrown up on the job yet," Abraham stopped when he came to the building's side. There was a hole in the brick wall as big as a refrigerator, and certainly wide enough for a man to squeeze through. Someone had tried to fix it, once upon a time, but the plywood over it had rotted and been chewed through. Whether it was a natural animal or something else, he couldn't be sure. Abraham stepped closer to investigate it, running his hand along the jagged brick line. "It isn't very well protected."

"Does it need to be?" Dracula scoffed. "Do you think anything that goes through there has a chance?"

"Fair point," Abraham gestured to the opening. "After you, sir."

Dracula sucked on his teeth and shaded his glasses with his hand as he peered inside. "Be sure to watch your step," he winked. "It is a little slippery right there." He set his foot inside and ground it against the floor before dragging it backward. A thick trail of blood stuck to his sole and followed him out until he smeared it on the grass.

"Fresh?" Abraham grabbed his crossbow by the sling.

"It certainly smells like it," the vampire rubbed at his nose.

"We've come this far," Abraham nudged him again with his elbow.

Dracula waved his hand dismissively, folding his black umbrella and ducking in through the entrance. Abraham followed suit, having to stoop a little lower to avoid knocking off his hat. His senses were immediately overwhelmed by the sharp smell of pennies, which was still barely strong enough to cover up the odor of what could have been open bowels.

Dracula scrunched up his nose in displeasure, but he kept his hand on his umbrella as they walked. Its pointed tip *'tapped'* against the concrete floor, and Abraham followed behind him as silently as he could manage in his tall, heeled boots.

They came in on the side of the main area where tables and chairs were jumbled together in precarious stacks. Some were broken and leaning heavily on their side while others looked like they had only recently been abandoned with wire baskets full of moldy potato wedges and overturned pints with shattered mouths.

There was so much broken glass on the pitch-black floor that it was almost as good as staring up at a clear night sky.

"I can't see a damn thing," Abraham muttered under his breath. "Can you?"

Dracula pinched the circle frames of his sunglasses and tilted his head back so he could glimpse the ceiling. "Not very much," he admitted. "You have a torch, don't you?"

"A flashlight?" Abraham flicked open a snap on his belt. "Yes."

"Well," Dracula waved his hand vaguely towards the ceiling.

Abraham slid the flashlight's lever all the way up the top and then flicked the beam towards the roof. All he caught in its bright yellow path was a tornado of dust motes spinning through the air. He moved the beam along slowly, the wavering circle slipping into nooks and crannies but not revealing anything helpful. Abraham kept it pointed upward as he started to move again, glass crunching underneath his heels a little louder than he would have liked.

"Keep your eye out," he said to his companion, "whatever is going to come will come fast."

"I am familiar," Dracula said with a hint of snark.

Abraham shifted his back teeth at the comment but tried to stay focused on the task at hand. "Mr. Dracula, I am going to need your cooperation."

"I have been *very* accommodating, *Mr. Helsing,*" Dracula hissed.

Dust fell. The sound of claws scraping over steel pipe was enough to silence them both as Abraham dragged his light over even further, seeking out the source. More dust fell as the creature above them seemed to move, and then the light glanced off a long gray tail that whipped through the air only momentarily before it curled back up and vanished. For the brief moment that Abraham saw it, it looked like a pile of sagging skin on top of a bulbous, dart-shaped end.

"It is up there," Abraham followed the creature with the light. He caught sight of a claw and a long, ragged ear. "Do you see it?"

"I see it," Dracula's lip curled. "It is hideous."

Abraham kept a tight grip on the flashlight as he grabbed his crossbow with his free hand and hefted it into the air. He had shot one-handed before, and it was not ideal. To use both hands he would have to lose sight of the creature, and there was no guarantee he would hit it then, either.

"I need you to drive it down," he had to keep himself from barking it out as an order. "I don't have a clear shot."

He had never asked Dracula to transform before. He had seen the vampire do it only a handful of times, with each escape that followed being narrower than the last. It was only ever when Dracula was angry – very, *very* angry.

Asking him to do it now felt like suicide – but if there were as many of these things nesting together as the vampire claimed, then a transformation was inevitable regardless.

"Oh, darling," even as Dracula smiled, the corners of his plum-colored mouth stretched impossibly wide to bare a set of sharp white teeth. His fangs had already doubled their length and he flicked his tongue between them, like a rattlesnake ready to strike. "Are you going to ask me nicely?"

"I do not have time for you," Abraham spit.

"Say please," Dracula peeled off his gloves. He grabbed his own fingers and pulled them until the cartilage snapped, stretching them out to accommodate an extra joint. "I want to hear you say it – *pretty please.*"

His nose turned upward, pushing itself back until the skin wrinkled between his eyes. His ears flattened and caved inward, resembling more a bat than anything else.

Abraham swallowed, fighting back a sudden wave of terror that made him realize he had no idea what he was asking for.

"Please," he breathed.

Dracula's delighted shriek became an animalistic screech. His legs folded into something inhuman and bent with talons like an eagle, which gave him all the more leverage as he sprang into the air. His claws dug into the beam where the gray creature was hiding, and he shook it. The structure shook with a rumbling groan, and Abraham felt a flash of concern that the whole building would come tumbling down around their heads. Dracula's large, leathery wings scraped the highest part of the ceiling's exposed infrastructure as he gained more momentum. The creature swiped an arm at him, and Dracula caught it by the hand. He flung it down towards the ground like a ragdoll and the creature tumbled, squalling, through the air.

Abraham dropped his flashlight so he could hold his crossbow with both hands. He hoisted it up locked his aim on the creature, tracking it through the scope.

With his first shot, it screamed, but the bolt only clipped its shoulder. It howled when it hit the ground and inky blood bubbled up from the deep wound. Abraham swore under his breath and aimed again. He had personally modified his crossbow so that it could shoot up to six bolts from a chamber before he needed to reload, but he was not eager to waste ammunition, especially when he did not know how many more could be waiting.

The creature swiveled its head until it was facing him. It stared at him with large yellow eyes that lit up its path like high beams on a dark highway. For half a second, it was very still, and his finger squeezed the trigger on his crossbow.

His vision was suddenly eclipsed by Dracula's wing as the vampire swept down from the ceiling and dug his claws into the hideous devil. Dracula pulled it apart as if it was made of paper, spraying black blood and clumps of guts across the room. Abraham pointed his crossbow upward to avoid hitting Dracula with the bolt, but he knew by the sound of the shrill, enraged shriek that he had not missed entirely.

Abraham glanced up. The bolt had driven a hole wide enough to put his fist through right in the center of Dracula's wing. The vampire looked at him, red eyes smoldering from behind a dark, shrouded brow.

He was a dead man if he did not leave.

Dracula raked his claw across the floor, scooping up blood and spilled entrails that were dismally scattered. He flung it at Abraham and hissed again as trails of bloody spittle streamed from his clenched jaw. Abraham backed up quickly, triggering the next round of his crossbow to load at the same time. A glob of something hit his face, and the smell was so vile that he almost vomited on the spot.

The crossed beams above their heads groaned again. A moment of stillness fell between them, and Abraham waited, not daring to take his eyes off Dracula's transformed figure.

After the moment had passed, the beams started to snap. The sound was deafening as one after the other splintered and gave out, showering dust and bits of wood to the floor. Abraham heard wood chips clattering against the brim of his hat as they fell.

The beams were soon joined by pipes. He heard the shrill sound of steel being wrenched apart and twisted around until it busted, followed quickly by the hiss of steam. A boiling white cloud formed quickly in the middle of the room, and from its center flew tens, dozens, *hundreds* more thrashing gray devils with floodlight eyes and dripping maws.

"Shit," Abraham raised his crossbow again. His next two rounds both struck through the chest. Two creatures reeled back, screaming as their flesh sizzled and black blood spurted from their pierced hearts. His next bolt only pierced one through the foot and sent it spinning. It crashed into another, and they both got caught in a stream of boiling water that sent them flying into a shattered beam, spearing them both on a ragged end.

Dracula was tearing them apart as quickly as they could fly at him. His hooked claws dug into their chests, breaking open their ribcages until the blood bubbled up and coated his hands. Some he ripped in half before sending the pieces flying in opposite directions, some he twisted off their heads like plastic dolls and crushed the skulls like eggshells in his massive hands. The skulls shattered in his iron grip without any trouble, spewing brain muck and yellow-white slime from the eye sockets.

Abraham's hand dove towards his belt. From one of the clips he pulled a string of glass grenades, each one cradled in a leather sleeve to protect them. The mercury gas inside was blessed – although how long it had been there, and by which Pope, he could not guess. Still holding onto his crossbow with one hand, he used the other to snap open the leather straps that kept them secured.

Once they were broken and the mercury was in the air, he was in just as much danger as the devils. The clock would be ticking for him, but they would have no chance.

He felt one of the grenades slide into his palm. Abraham hurled it towards the throng and heard it shatter as it hit the floor. A cacophony of screams rose into the air as the creatures started spinning, shrieking and tearing at their own skin.

He went for another, and realized he had forgotten about Dracula.

"Goddamn it!" He called out. "Mr. Dracula, I do not mean to concern you, but it would be within your best interests to run!"

He threw another grenade down. The glass exploded the creatures caught within its cloud were spiraling faster. Some of them dropped to the floor like stoned crows, others were tearing off their thick gray skin in gory sheets.

The blood on the floor was as slick as oil. Abraham grabbed six more silver bolts from their holster and used them to reload his crossbow's chamber. He gave it a spin and then held it high once again, looking through the scope to see which of the bastards he would be able to nail next.

He fired again, and again – catching one through the throat and the other right through the roof of its gaping mouth. The blessed mercury was doing its job, with more and more of the creatures falling down around him.

He could hardly see a thing, now, between the steam and his own blurring vision. The gas was making his head spin, and holding up the crossbow made him feel like he was going to tip over.

"Fuck," he closed one eye altogether and tried to limit his use to its twin. The creatures were barreling through the air in all directions, falling, flapping, spasming – bursting.

He could not see what caused him to fall, all Abraham knew was that suddenly he was going down. He tried to reach out and grab onto something – anything – but the only thing his hand landed on was a broken skull like a putrid orange. That foul, acrid stench filled his nose once again and he couldn't help the fountain of vomit that surged up his throat and spewed from his mouth and nose. Abraham's hands slid across the floor as he tried to pull himself upright, but each time he attempted to rise, pain shot up his leg and sent him right back down. His vision went completely white. The pain was so staggering that he just trying to shift onto his hip made him feel like he had to vomit again.

More wings flapping around him, more devils screaming and squabbling. This was the end of the line, for him.

Something slid underneath him, lifting him up off the floor with ease as if he weighed no more than a bobcat. Through the stench of devil's blood he catch the faint scent of Dracula's cologne – like dried-up roses and deadnettle.

"Now, Mr. Helsing," Dracula sounded entirely like himself again, and not the monster he had transformed into. "What a mess you have created."

Abraham groaned. Everything he wanted to say was on the tip of his tongue, but it felt too swollen to move and too large for his mouth.

Dracula clucked his tongue. Abraham felt too heavy to pull away and protest, yet strangely weightless as the vampire carried him out. He retained his consciousness just long enough to feel cool air hit his face as they exited – presumably the way they came.

A loud boom sounded off behind them, enough to make his heart race despite how he could not keep his eyes open. He could smell smoke, and the roar of quickly climbing flames was not enough to drown out the screams of the damned that were being consumed.

4

Amigraine, like a tent-spike being driven through his temple, was what woke him up. A warm breeze slipped its fingers through the holes in his window screen and tickled the bristly stubble on his chin while bringing faint outdoor smells that were enough to trigger his nausea. Abraham dug his fingers into his eyes, rubbing out the sand until all the crust had flaked away and he could peel back his eyelids enough to check the time. His vision was bleary, and the flashing red numbers on his digital clock were just a row of eights and zeroes. Clearly, it had come unplugged at some point, or the power had flipped off altogether.

Not that the time was important. It was dark outside, and that was all he needed to know. Hours did not mean anything to him once the sun went down.

He had no memory of returning home. His mouth tasted like blood, and behind his pulsing migraine there was a faint recollection of flames and devils screaming. The air was drier than a bone, and he could not quite brush off the wave of irritation that hit him when he saw the off-white slats of his blinds pushed up. He never slept with the window open – there were too many different *things* out there that wanted him dead.

Abraham tried to sit up. As soon as he shifted his leg, another wave of pain shot up to the top of his thigh and stabbed him in the hip. He diffused a curse through his teeth and gave himself a moment to breathe through it, his breath trembling as he waited for the jolt to fade into an ache. He tried to move again, this time by driving his knuckles into the mattress to let his arms do the lion's share of the lifting. The pain hit him again and he gave up, swearing loudly as he fell hard against his pillows and almost knocked his head against the wall.

"Look at you," Dracula's tongue curled around his thick Romanian vowels, distinguishable even when Abraham was half-asleep. "Is this what they mean when they talk about 'breakfast in bed'?"

Abraham could not help but huff. "Are you going to eat me, then?" He was only slightly worried. Between his migraine and the pain in his leg, death would not have been an unwelcome development.

Dracula laughed. He moved closer to the bed while the shadows pulled away from him like the dramatic reveal of a cloak. The flashing red light from the alarm clock granted a Warholian quality to his gnarled-lavender skin. "I am joking, of course," he said. "I do not *eat* anyone. I drink their blood until they are dead."

"Pedantic," Abraham grunted.

"I had a very good opportunity to suck you dry already, and I did not," Dracula flashed his pearly white fangs as his smile grew. "So, not only have you lost your sense of humor, but you are also ungrateful."

"Are you telling me that you saved my life?" He believed that, but he did not know how to feel about it. "Why would you do that?"

"Consider it a modest act of good faith, a repayment for services rendered—even if they *were* a sort of consolidation on a debt," Dracula sat down on the edge of the bed, walking his long black nails up the thin rumpled cover. "I would consider us, now, to be on even ground."

"Bullshit," Abraham said, "it is not that simple."

"Shall I complicate it further? Because when you die in my arms, Mr. Helsing, it is going to be on my terms." The vampire's blood-red eyes reflected white in the darkness like a lurking crocodile. He drew his hand up and rested it against Abraham's bare chest. His icy touch sent a graveyard chill down to Abraham's lungs, slowing the draw on his following breath. "What can I say? I am not ready to let you go."

Fear formed a ball of ice in Abraham's throat and he swallowed it down. He had been alone with Dracula many times before, but it had never been like this. It was not the first time he had been wounded, but it was the first time that he had been bedridden with such a powerful vampire eyeing him like a barred owl with a garter snake. The invitation into his house had been opened, and Dracula would not leave until it was revoked – yet, if Abraham sent him out before understanding the extent of the damage that had been done, then there was no way of knowing when help would be able to come. The hospital was a good 45 minutes away, and he could hardly even move. He did not know where his phone was. He did not have neighbors who would come by to check on his well-being. All he had was Quincey – and the dog was not even in the room.

He was trapped, and vulnerable, and Dracula knew it. That was why he kept the window open – because even if Abraham screamed, there would be no one around to hear it.

Abraham's breath was not coming any steadier, and his arms were starting to shake from the exertion of holding him upright.

"If you are not going to kill me," Abraham said, "may I trouble you for a glass of water?"

"Oh, yes," Dracula said as if that had all somehow slipped his mind. "I brought something for you, and these." He dropped a few white pills into Abraham's palm. "I found them above your fridge."

Abraham brought the pills close to his face to inspect them. "What was on the label?"

"I did not look, but I am sure they will help," Dracula said. "Modern medicine is amazing but it all sort of does the same thing, doesn't it?"

"I can assure you that it does not," Abraham told him. He brought the pills a little closer to his face for inspection. They looked like Tylenol – and if they turned out not to be, well – then if he died, he died.

Dracula passed him a glass of orange juice that tasted like it had been in the fridge for just a little too long, but Abraham tried not to think about it as he knocked the pills back.

"You did a number on your leg," the vampire said. "I did the best that I could with it, but I do not think you will be getting out of bed anytime soon. Much less slaying monsters." He rolled the word *'monsters'* around in his mouth like it was something salacious. Abraham grunted and tried to adjust himself again to be comfortable, careful not to jostle his leg.

"What you are saying is that I am a sitting duck," he said. "Would you mind closing the window?"

"Oh, Mr. Helsing, what are you afraid of?" Dracula stood up anyway and walked over to the window. He grabbed it by the lip and jerked it down while it made a loud snapping sound in protest.

"Are you saying that you are already the most dangerous thing in the room?" Abraham closed his eyes. His vision was starting to swim again and all the talking was not helping his head. "I think I would agree."

"I would say that perhaps, I am the one with my head about me," Dracula said. "For instance, you would not have caught me *dead* throwing mercury into the air without a mask of some sort. It does make me wonder if you are going senile a little early. The Helsings were always a touch premature." He flicked his tongue over his fangs.

Abraham scoffed under his breath and did not comment on that.

"The matter of your senility, of course, had me thinking about your grandfather—which has led me to be more than a little reminiscent while waiting for you to regain consciousness," Dracula's r's rolled grandly off his tongue as he walked around the foot of Abraham's bed. "You will have to forgive me if I get a little sentimental on you."

"Mmm?" Abraham slid his hand over his eye again. "I've got time." He said dryly.

Dracula cackled. "Of course you do," he said. The quality of his voice softened into that rich, luring tone tailor-made for seduction. "I could not help but notice, as I was rifling through your things, that you kept your grandfather's crucifix."

Abraham paused, grinding the heel of his hand into his eye socket. A little deeper and he could end his own misery. "You were going through my things?"

"It is in sorry shape, but all things considered – I think it is holding up well." The vampire flashed his fangs.

Abraham let out a slow breath. "What did you try to do with it?"

"Oh, do not get so bent out of shape," Dracula huffed. "I did not touch the filthy thing." He wriggled his fingers, barely visible now in the darkness. "It is not as if I can."

"I have a picture of him, somewhere. Why don't you go through my bibles and see if you can find it?" Abraham said through his teeth.

"You are not nearly so polite when you are in unimaginable pain," Dracula did not even try to cover his revelry. "And I have an excellent memory, as you are very well-aware. I don't think a little black-and-white snapshot is going to compare to the living color reels I keep in my head of that man." His luminescent red eyes turned back towards Abraham. "He was a proud gentleman of well-established German ancestry. Very distinguished. You look absolutely nothing like him."

Abraham managed a glare. "So I've been told," he snapped.

"And he came all the way over here just to end the line. At least you can add poor follow-through to your list of inherited qualities."

The last thing that Abraham wanted to do was fight with an incurable maniac. The second-last thing he wanted to do was talk about his grandfather. Helsing Sr. had been dead for almost eleven years. More than a decade, but it still stung, and he did not have any whiskey to drown out his feelings on the matter.

"If you are going to keep talking like this," Abraham said, "I am going to need a stiffer drink."

"Oh, Mr. Helsing," Dracula's words were like a prayer, "I would give it to you, but I do not much like the taste of alcohol. It thins the blood, and I am not a messy eater."

Understanding dawned on Abraham, and the brutal clarity of what could be no more blatantly stated somewhat relieved the tension in his head. "So, what is this?"

"Consider this something of your eleventh hour," Dracula said. "Do you wish to make any confessions?"

"I thought you said you were not going to kill me," Abraham told him.

Dracula held up a finger. "I believe what I said was – you will die on *my* terms. That could be now, it could be in another decade. Although there is a difference between finely-aged and soured, and I believe you are toeing the line."

"Meanwhile, we are both going to sit here and let you ruminate for a spell?" Abraham could not help a short, dry laugh. "All right. So, I am to accept that if you do not drink my blood tonight, there is always the night after, or the night after that. My time is being borrowed."

Dracula clattered his fingernails together. "Would you say that the anticipation is just *killing* you?"

Abraham rolled his eyes upward until they ached. "God has my confession," he said. "The Devil does not need it too."

"Have you considered," Dracula ran his fingers down the front of his fine shirt, "that only the Devil is interested in what you have to say?"

"If you are trying to say something like God has turned his back on me, then I believe it," the pain was ebbing away as the meds kicked in, but Abraham was still uncomfortable.

"No," Dracula said, "nothing so trite."

"I am tired," Abraham sighed. "There is a confession for you. Am I going to be allowed to sleep, or are you going to keep me up all night with your badgering?"

"Well, I cannot very well pay you a visit in the morning, now can I?" Dracula asked. "It does distress me to think that you might lie awake for so many hours without a way to eat or relieve yourself. I would not drink so much orange juice."

Abraham made a face. "I will manage," he said. "I have had worse."

"I am certain that you have," Dracula's voice was a sigh, and he disappeared altogether in the darkness. Abraham could no longer see even the outline of his

profile, and the air smelled like a snuffed match.
"Goodnight, Mr. Helsing. Sleep well. Do not allow
me to disturb you."

5

braham dreamt of his grandfather, even though he could barely remember his face.

He dreamt that he saw Helsing Sr. in the kitchen with a tall glass of milk and a tin of shortbread cookies resting on the counter. Abraham could tell that his grandfather was dead because his hands were mottled and his eyes were the same milky silver color as a fish on ice at the supermarket—but Helsing Sr. did not seem to notice. His discolored hands were covered in ugly black stitches, and he rocked back and forth on his heels as if he had too much fluid in his head to keep his balance. Abraham could hear gospel records being played from the living room— some old quartet he once knew the name of, but could not recall now. He could not understand the words, if there were any, to the songs. It was all jumbled and he decided it was German.

His grandfather looked like he was going to fall over. Helsing Sr. leaned back on his heels until his head was nearly touching the low-hanging light over the sink. Abraham reached for him, but a jolt of pain shot up his leg and stopped him from going any further.

He tried for every word—*großvater, sir*—but they all stuck in his throat. The only sound that came out was a moan, as if his jaw was slack and incapable of forming anything intelligible. Another jab of pain and Abraham woke up, finding himself in a position where he was half-hanging off the bed and holding himself up from the floor with his palms pressed against the wooden boards. The bedsheets were tangled around his wounded leg, and the pain climbed all the way up his spine.

Abraham pushed against the floor and performed a minor acrobatic feat in order to get himself back into bed. His hips and his back crackled as he did so and he grasped the edge of his bedside table in order to give himself some leverage. He grabbed hold of the clock and slid it closer to him—but of course, it was still flashing. Dracula had never reset it.

There was a little light coming from the windows, but it was the dark piss-yellow of a waning sun. He had slept through most of the day – which was not surprising, all things considered. The only thing he really had going for him was the fact that his migraine was mostly gone.

He could still feel it lingering in the center of his skull, like someone was tapping on the sorest spot with a screwdriver. The agony in his leg was almost blinding, but he had been so intent on not falling that he had been able to ignore it. Now that he was back in bed, he felt it more than before, his vision swam a little. He worked on breathing through it, trying to focus instead on other things.

His mouth was dry, and he wanted water. That was all he could think about, but it was something.

A wet glass touched his fingertips. Abraham looked over and saw Dracula standing by the bed, his red circle glasses covering his eyes against the waning sunlight. Whatever was left of the day only remained at the very bottom of the bed, and the rest of the room was cast in a watery gray shadow.

"I brought some water for you," Dracula said, showing all his pearly white teeth. "You look a little dry."

"Thank you," Abraham muttered. He struggled into a sitting position and threw himself against his headboard, grabbing the glass and draining it without another word. Dracula picked up his alarm clock in the meantime, flipping it over and playing with the dials on the back.

"I suppose I should reset this for you," Dracula said. Abraham shrugged.

"I hate to trouble you," he said. "Is there food still in this house?"

"I believe that there might be," Dracula set the alarm clock down. The numbers were still all eights, but it was no longer flashing. "Are you hungry?"

"Peckish," Abraham admitted. He could not remember the last time he eaten. He was accustomed to going without meals, but after a good twelve hours, his stomach knew to complain.

"I daresay that I am famished," Dracula slid his sunglasses down his sharp nose and his eyes roamed over Abraham's supine form. Abraham tensed, suddenly aware of the faint patch of daylight that was slipping farther down his covers with every passing second.

"Well," Abraham said, "I would ask that you feel free to help yourself, however."

Dracula flicked his tongue over one pointed fang. "You are catching on quickly to what I can do when given the invitation."

"I would never," Abraham's breath escaped on a rasp, "make the same mistake twice."

"Thrice," Dracula's fingers landed against his shoulder, raising chill bumps on his hot bare skin. "Perhaps more, but who is really keeping count? Not you, clearly."

Abraham ground his teeth. "I must have been in a trance of some sort," he said, "I know that hypnosis is part of your particular brand of bedevilment."

"That is true," Dracula's eyes glittered. "Although I have never needed to use it on *you*. Not after the first time."

"Bullshit!" Abraham's lip curled and he turned his head. Dracula grabbed his chin and pulled his head back around, purple hands seizing his throat with an elegant thumb stroking the swell of his larynx.

"There is no need for such language," Dracula said. "Why take my word for it? It is easily proven."

Abraham swallowed. He felt his salty, sticky skin press against Dracula's thumb. "Verona," he said. Even to his own ears, his voice sounded hoarse.

"Verona," Dracula purred. "Bonnie Tyler."

"Red wine, for me," Abraham continued. "Red wine and *torta delle rose*. It was such a strange night."

"You were out of your mind," Dracula laughed softly in the growing dark. "You were so inebriated that you told me to taste it."

"You said…" Abraham did not want the sudden onslaught of memories. He closed his eyes as if that could shut them out.

"Go on," Dracula urged him.

"You said you could taste them off my tongue," he opened his eyes again. "You *bit* my tongue."

"It was not entirely a lie, then," Dracula said. "And you had no protests as to what came after."

"A great many mistakes," Abraham said. His breath ached in his chest.

"One right after the other, like nails in a coffin," Dracula's smile grew. "You were almost mine. I nearly had you."

"I came out of it," Abraham did not meet the vampire's eyes. He kept his gaze fixed on Dracula's nose, but he felt like it was too late—like the vampire had already put him under some sort of spell. "You waited too long. I would count that an error on your part."

"Perhaps I was not done with you," Dracula said. "I never could resist the call for one final dance before the music stopped and the candles were put out."

"Is that what you came here to do?" Abraham asked. "Was that your intent from the beginning? Are you going to put out the candle?"

"No, Mr. Helsing," Dracula leaned in a little closer, "not without a final dance."

He was so close that Abraham could smell his cologne. Dried-up roses and spice like Catholic church incense. He could smell the blood underneath it, too, a fresh kill that was betrayed by the slight tinge of pink on those pearly-white fangs. Dracula had fed recently—and Abraham could only hope it was not anyone he knew.

The whites of the vampire's eyes were flushed and his pale lavender skin was almost maroon on the apples of his cheeks. His lips were plum-red, alive, and while his hands were still cold – they were no longer like ice.

"Where is Quincey?" Abraham breathed. Dracula's lips were so close to his own that when he spoke, they almost touched.

"Do not worry, Mr. Helsing, I did not eat your dog." The tip of Dracula's black fingernails dragged along the soft underside of Abraham's chin and tilted his head up. The vampire's long, red tongue snaked out and dragged its way along Abraham's bottom lip, then pushed itself past the barrier and filled the hunter's mouth. Abraham did not fight against it—he opened his mouth willingly, letting Dracula push his tongue down his throat until he choked around it. Abraham reached up and grabbed the front of the vampire's shirt. All he could feel underneath was hard, undead flesh—nothing living or inviting at all, and yet, it was familiar.

Over the past thirty years, Abraham had not been able to find satisfaction in a warm, living creature. And whether that was bewitchment, or something within him that he was not ready to confront—he did not know. When Dracula overtook him, something primal was always released. It was a deep-seated hunger fueled by a reckless sense of abandonment. Death lost all meaning on a vampire's tongue. Dracula's teeth, his hands, his mouth—all worked in tandem to devour Abraham without taking a morsel out of his flesh. The vampire could have him, body and soul, again and again without ever leaving a mark—except for the searing pain in the cavity of Abraham's chest, like a sizzling brand left on his heart that converted into white-hot agony whenever it was all said and done.

He had studied enough lore to know that that meant something—but he had never examined it too closely. He did not want to. There was a degree of freedom in giving the oldest known vampire in the world exactly his way, while not asking too many questions.

Dracula pulled back, and Abraham followed him as if pulled by a string. The vampire placed his hand around Abraham's throat again, dragging his tongue along his jawline, drawing a wet path all the way up to his ear where he paused, and he whispered, "I believe that you have something for me?"

Although the pressure on his throat was light, Abraham could barely breathe. "Yes," it was not a question anymore. The time for fighting back had passed.

He could hear the smile in Dracula's voice, even though he could not see it. "I do not think a simple 'yes' will do."

Abraham closed his eyes. He wanted to beg not to have to say the words, as much as he wanted to plead with them until his tongue bled. *"Bitte, mein herr."*

He always felt like his accent butchered the words, but a velvety purr rolled up and down Dracula's throat in approval.

"Băiat bun," the pompous inflection dropped from his voice when he used his old Romanian tongue. He said it again, and this time Abraham understood. "Good boy."

Abraham's hands went down to his hips. He was still wearing his jeans from the day before and felt slightly self-conscious about their grimy state. Dracula made him feel that way—grimy, in the presence of something so stately and striking. He was vaguely aware of his own pain, but Dracula's dark, alluring words and his cool, commanding touch banished most of it into the back of his brain. Abraham pushed his jeans down and managed to toss them to the floor. His heavy belt buckle hit the wood with a dull thud.

"It has been some time," Abraham breathed, as if Dracula did not know.

"I am sure you will warm up to it," Dracula's fingers wandered down, skating over the hunter's sensitive inner thighs and pausing to squeeze his groin. "It looks like it is already coming back to you."

Abraham licked his lips. His chest burned with threatening heat as Dracula pulled away, only quelled by the fact that the vampire was not leaving, and that he was only sinking further down along the bed. Dracula parted Abraham's thighs and ran his hands down the length of his wounded legs. Abraham hissed in pain, a sound which converted into a cry as Dracula grabbed his shins and pushed them upward, forcing his swollen knees to bend.

"Does that hurt?" The vampire asked innocently. Abraham nodded, unable to stutter out a word beyond the pain and his own heady need.

"Wonderful," Dracula whispered. He slid his fingers down—beautiful fingers, long and slender, bearing heavy antique rings embedded with glittering jewels. The rings alone were probably worth more than half the oil rigs in Texas put together. Abraham felt them against his most intimate place. He held his breath and shot his gaze towards the roof, grabbing the thin cotton sheets underneath him as if they alone could act as an anchor.

Dracula's nails were razor-sharp. It was more of a knifing than a loving penetration. Abraham could feel his own hot blood start to flow. It dripped down his sphincter and soaked the sheets underneath. Dracula persisted, inserting one finger at first, and then two. He worked himself all the way up to three before he decided that that was enough, pushing them as deep as they could go—until his rings were rammed up against the tight ring of muscle like a battering ram, and then he kept pushing. Abraham ground his teeth against the pain, nearly biting his own tongue in half when he felt the rings. Dracula drove his fingers inside all the way up to the third knuckle, rings and all. Abraham was bleeding profusely, he could smell it better than he could feel it.

Dracula pulled his hand back at last, not bothering to be gentle. His fingers were shiny with blood, completely coated. It looked black underneath the moonlight that was pouring in through the window. Abraham felt compelled to look at the vampire again, and his gaze was immediately arrested by those dark red eyes, which stared him down as Dracula raised his hand to his mouth and sucked the blood away from his own fingers.

"How does it feel, Abraham?" Dracula's voice slithered through the darkness even though his mouth did not form the words.

"Like Hell," Abraham replied hoarsely. "Like sitting on the mouth of Hell and looking down to see the bottom."

"Do you mean to say that it hurts?" Dracula leaned over his body. He placed the tips of his wet fingers against Abraham's mouth and prompted him to open up. Abraham did as he was silently bid, and Dracula slid his fingers inside. All Abraham could taste was his own blood.

"Uhh," Abraham could not get any words out around the vampire's fingers. Dracula pushed them deeper inside until they touched the very back of the hunter's tongue. Abraham choked again, feeling his throat contract around Dracula's hand. He fought against his own desire to submit—to let Dracula roll him with his eyes, to become mindless, like so many other humans he had seen who gave their will over to such creatures.

"It hurts a little more now than it used to, does it not?" Dracula whispered, his bloody mouth pressed to Abraham's ear. "As you get older, it keeps getting worse. Think how much pain you are in now, and then how it will increase tenfold by the next time we dance. That is the thing about years, Abraham. They pile on your chest like stone slabs until they steal your breath away."

"Ahh," Dracula's fingers slid out of Abraham's mouth, and he drooled down his chin, but he still could not answer.

"Eternity," Dracula continued, "does not hurt nearly as much."

"*Herr…*" Abraham struggled to breathe. "Vladislav."

"You can taste it, can't you? Close your eyes," Dracula's nails pulled on his cheek. "I think you will find that death can taste a little bit like *torta delle rose.*"

Abraham could see it—Verona. Dracula probably did not remember it like he did. The city had so many lights that the streets looked like it had been flooded with stars, and was so bright that the moon shielded herself with clouds. The *torta delle rose* was not the only dish he tried, but he remembered it because he had liked it best. The red wine, too, a departure from his usual whiskey or bourbon. At one point, he had tried to get Dracula to drink from his glass. The vampire had laughed in his face.

He did not remember how they ended up there, on the second story balcony of a little café that probably did not exist anymore. All Abraham could remember was the feeling in the pit of his stomach—something about feeling like, somewhere, the roles had been reversed—and he was the one being hunted.

Panic broke through the sublime submission that was rolling over his skin in warm, golden waves. It granted him enough clarity that he felt the pain in his leg through it, and his entire body jolted.

"Fermare!" He called out in—Italian, probably— it did not matter. He drove his hand against Dracula's chest to put some kind of wedge between them. He was panting, Abraham realized. His chest was heaving, and his skin was clammy—as sure as if he had been running.

"Cosa?" Dracula paused and humored him with a smile.

The expression did not make it all the way up to the vampire's eyes. The good humor died at the corners of his sharp mouth.

"Stop it," Abraham gasped out the words. "Stop it! Enough. Enough!"

Dracula held up his hands, although he did not move from between Abraham's legs. "I have stopped," the vampire said. There was an edge to his voice.

"I am not…" Abraham brought a hand to his face. He had not realized how violently he was trembling. If Dracula pulled away from him entirely, he felt like he would fall to pieces. His chest burned, and the pain was so intense that he was afraid of vomiting froth if he moved. "I am not a toy for you to play with."

"Of course not," Dracula said. "I am not a child. I do not stick my toys in my mouth."

"I am not your next meal, either" Abraham dragged himself back up, although he was still bleeding—and now his thighs were sticky, and his rectum hurt. "I want you out of my house."

"Are you revoking your invitation?" Dracula's tongue swiped across his lips like a cat, but he did not move otherwise. His eyes reflected the moonlight, flashing white in the darkness—a waiting predator.

For a moment, Abraham froze. He took quick stock of his situation and determined that if he was going to die—he would deserve it—but he would at least not be naked.

"I am," he snapped. "Get out. Even Southern hospitality can only go so far."

It was all words, now. The rules of hospitality—Southern or folkoric—no longer applied. Every illusion had been torn down, and now they were exactly as they had always been—predator and prey, although Abraham now had to face the gutting reality of which he had become.

"I daresay," now Dracula was mocking his Texas accent, "I do not take kindly to being dismissed." Even as he spoke, the vampire's red eyes bled to black like spreading pools of ink. He opened his mouth and Abraham heard the hinges of his jaw pop.

It was time to go. Adrenaline took over. Gritting his teeth through the pain, Abraham pulled his legs out from underneath the count and dove towards the floor. He grabbed his jeans and pulled them on, snapping the belt buckle in place as he ran. He ran through his inventory in his head, trying to think of the nearest stash where he could grab something to defend himself. There were a couple of short wooden stakes in his top dresser drawer, but he had already left those behind. The next closest things were the strings of garlic hanging in his pantry and his jar full of black salt. Minor wards, but they could keep Dracula at bay.

Not for long—not in a 1300 square foot house— but it could give him a leg up, at least. Abraham darted for the kitchen. He heard Quincey whine but he could not see his dog. He glanced out the small window that was above the sink and saw the hound jumping up at the windowsill, whimpering and scratching to get in. There was no way of knowing how long he had been outside, either. It was probably for the best, in this case, but Abraham made a mental note to be angry about it later. He pulled open the pantry door, ripping down a string of garlic bulbs just in time for the vampire to catch up with him.

Abraham turned around, using the momentum to slam his fist into Dracula's face. The garlic bulbs, which were a little old, caved and smeared against the vampire's skin. A dark hiss streamed through Dracula's teeth as he grabbed Abraham's wrist with such force that the bone felt like it was going to snap. Abraham fought against the pain and brought his free hand up to drive his knuckles against the vampire's cold, carved cheekbone. Dracula released his hold, and Abraham crushed some more of the garlic in his hands until the juices stung the cuts on his palm and the papery, thin skin showered to the floor from between his fingers. He stuffed the ruined cloves into Dracula's open mouth and the count's tongue released a thick plume of white steam. Black blood, like oil, dribbled out of his mouth and coated Abraham's hand.

Dracula's shoulders hunched forward, and he cupped his hand underneath his chin to catch the blood. He rolled his eyes up to look at Abraham, his mouth contorting into something resembling a smile, and he flashed his slime-covered teeth.

"Mr. Helsing," he said, gargling more blood as he spoke, "we can work this out."

"Every time," Abraham spit, "you say it every time."

"I said it to your grandfather, he did not believe me either," Dracula's smile stretched wider. "Although I must say—of your whole line, you are the *first* Helsing to tango so closely with me."

"Is that so?" He had heard stories. Now was not the time to discuss them.

"It really is a shame that you do not trust me."

The chair he had broken a day or two before was still propped on top of the kitchen table where he had set it to keep it off the floor. Abraham grabbed it by a hanging rung and ripped the wood free. A hail of splinters flew towards Dracula's face and the vampire threw his arm up to his shield his eyes. Abraham held up the makeshift stake until it was level with Dracula's chest, gripping it so tightly that his knuckles turned white.

Dracula laughed, darting his long tongue over his teeth and sweeping up the dark blood that glistened on his fangs. "I can smell you," he lowered his voice. "You have blood dripping down your legs."

"You have blood under your nails," Abraham countered, trying to keep his breath even.

"You have spent your entire life in this dance with me," Dracula began to pace. He circled Abraham like a jungle cat and Abraham followed his movements, pivoting on the ball of his heel to match the vampire's smooth, precise steps. "There is still time to let the Devil hear your confession."

Abraham scowled. "I have nothing to say."

Dracula's expression rippled, as if his amusement was quickly waning. "The Devil has His ways of knowing. Or did you think that I would not find out about what you said to your preacher?"

Abraham's heart stopped in his chest. For a moment, he thought he was dead, because he could not remember how to breathe.

"Were you there?" His hand burned from where he was gripping the torn wood. Any tighter and it would shatter in his hands. "Then how could you know?"

"Truth will out, as the bards say," Dracula cackled. "Now, we can try again—"

"I have revoked my invitation. And I want you *out* of my house!" Abraham's heart started up again with a painful jolt, and he drove the makeshift stake forward towards the vampire's chest. Dracula dodged, spinning on the gleaming toes of his shoes across the linoleum. Abraham clutched his chest. He still felt like he could not breathe.

He followed the vampire into the living room. The stench of death was heavy, there. It shoved a balled-up fist into Abraham's mouth to where it was all he could taste on the back of his tongue. He turned his eyes immediately to the couch, where he saw a dark figure slumped over the arm.

It was a body—long dead, from the look and smell of it. The neck was torn apart, viciously, as if the victim had been attacked by a coyote. Abraham took a single step closer—he did not need a good look at the face to recognize who it was.

"Your preacher came calling, I think he was worried about you," Dracula said. "His jugular babbled like a brook—and told me all sorts of stories about you."

Dracula seized his hand from behind. Abraham kept his grip on the stake as he swung around to try and wrench himself free, but Dracula was stronger. The vampire dragged him down and slammed his hand into the coffee table. It hit wood the first time, and Abraham clenched his teeth in pain. The second time, it hit a glass candy dish, and the dish broke apart on contact. The thick green glass sliced into Abraham's hand and he cried out in pain, releasing his hold on the makeshift stake until it rolled off the side of the coffee table and onto the ground.

With his hand free, Abraham scooped up a handful of the broken glass. He flung it at Dracula's face and the vampire let out a chilling, preternatural shriek. Abraham threw himself back, landing on the floor, and dug his heels into the carpet to give him some leverage to crawl backwards. His hand felt like it was on fire, but his adrenaline dulled the pain. Dracula was staring at him, all red eyes and bared, bloodied fangs. The aristocrat was leaving, and the creature was taking over. Abraham felt his heart in his throat.

"Helsing," Dracula's voice had blended into something darker, and it no longer sounded like the one that Abraham knew. The vampire could hardly speak around his own slavering mouth. "Come closer."

Abraham's hands shook as he reached above his head. He grabbed the wires of his record player and tugged, grabbing the edge of the table it sat on to try and pull himself up at the same time. Dracula's gaze was trying to pull him. If he made eye contact now it would all be lost. He felt it—he wanted to, he *needed* to—it would be easy, giving in. It would be a relief.

'And it will not hurt,' Dracula's voice slithered over the inside of his skull, *'not one bit'.*

Abraham pulled on the cords again. The record player slid into his hands.

'Trust me, Helsing.'

Abraham stood up at last. His legs shook as his knees felt too weak to support him and he leaned against the table, clutching the sides of the record player.

'Look at me.'

"No!" Abraham ground his teeth. Dracula hissed, and the voice in Abraham's head resonated.

'LOOK AT ME!'

Abraham's hands were slick with blood. He gripped the record player as tightly as he could, afraid of dropping it as he raised it above his head. He swung it down, yelling until his throat was raw, and bashed it into the side of the count's head. Dracula screamed, and Abraham hit him again—not sure about which parts of the vampire he was making contact with, but satisfied that he was beating him back at all.

Dracula rolled across the floor. A shock of black blood streamed down the side of his face and disappeared into his high collar. Abraham swung the record player at him again and lost his grip. It bounced off the vampire's shoulder and Abraham picked it up by the cords. The record player groaned and he felt like he was going to lose it, but he managed to double the cord around his fingers and bring it up, swinging it again until it connected with Dracula's temple.

His vision was going white with pain, from his busted leg to his gushing hands. He heard popping joints break the sudden fall of silence—a familiar enough sound. Dracula was going to transform.

"Not here," Abraham whispered and spat onto the floor. He would rather end it all, now, than go through it all again in another five, six—or ten years. How long would Dracula spend, chasing him down until he could not fight back? He had been a witness to this game his whole life. He had seen what it did to his grandfather.

"Not here," he repeated it under his breath like a prayer. More popping, more groaning. He was running out of time. He picked up the bottle of whiskey that rested on the coffee table, turned over on its side from all the ruckus. He grabbed it and darted his eyes over every surface of the room, where they finally came to rest on his bookshelf.

On the shelf, sitting on top of the warped cover of his grandfather's bible and right next to a copy of *The Divine Comedy,* was a crumpled pack of Marlboro's. Abraham dove for it, covering the short distance quickly with bloody footprints that seeped into the carpet. He grabbed the pack and shook out a cheap green lighter. It looked a little low on fluid, but he prayed it would be enough.

He looked over at Dracula, hardly able to get a full view through his hazy vision. Abraham twisted off the metal cap to the whiskey bottle and tossed it aside. He took a swig and it burned his lacerated mouth like hellfire.

The rest he poured out. Abraham flung a line of whiskey between himself and Dracula and then crouched down, flicking on the lighter. He hesitated only a second before catching the soaked patch of carpet with the flame. It caught almost immediately, smoking and then blazing. It tore across the room, spreading quickly—the house was old. The whole damn thing would catch fire, sure as preaching.

And if there was one thing Abraham knew about vampires, it was that they lit up quicker than a match.

Smoke filled the room, starting gray and going black. Abraham could no longer see Dracula, but he could hear the vampire moving. He heard something scrabbling against the walls, like a rat being flushed out of a gutter. Abraham made the sign of the cross and staggered for his back door. Quincey was whining and barking on the other side, driven to a frenzy by the commotion and the smoke.

'Helsing,' the voice filled his head. *'It is not so easy.'*

Abraham swallowed. His head spun. The pain, the loss of blood—if he made it to his truck, it would be a miracle.

"Get out of my head," he slammed his knee into the back door to get it to open faster. "Get out of my goddamn head!"

Smoke followed him out on the back porch. Quincey ran up to him but did not jump. The hound whimpered in concern, and Abraham extended a hand to his dog. He kept walking—too afraid to stop.

He had no idea of the time, but the sky was still pitch black. If Dracula made it out past the fire, then it would be over. He did not feel like he had any fight left in him.

He just had to make it to his truck. His bad leg started to drag, and Helsing had to reach down and grab his thigh to keep himself moving. It had gone from excruciating pain to quickly losing all feeling. He knew that was bad, but as long as he could still drive—it was something he could worry about later.

The door was unlocked. It was always unlocked. He kept a spare car key under the mat for reasons such as this. He worried less about it getting stolen and more about quick escapes. He could always replace a truck.

Quincey jumped in without prompting. Abraham looked over his shoulder. Through the windows he could see the orange glow of flame as it quickly overtook everything inside. He expected to see something else—wings, a creature—something, anything, to come breaking through the roof or the windows or even the side.

There was nothing. He did not hear anything—no breaking glass, no roars, no screams.

Abraham's hand shook as he plunged his key into the ignition and slammed the truck door shut. His engine heaved angrily and he flicked on the headlights, half-expecting to see Dracula standing in his driveway, covered in blood and ash.

Nothing, still. And he did not find that comforting. He needed a body. He needed to be sure that Dracula was gone.

Unless he went back into the house, there would be no way to know for sure.

That would be suicide.

He knew that he was being taunted. Hunted, still, by this generational parasite. Dracula was using his silence to lure Abraham back in. Even without taking the bait, Abraham would still be left to wonder—and he would spend days, weeks, months looking over his shoulder at every turn. Now, of course, his home was a lost cause. He had nowhere to go. The vampire had flushed him out of the tall grass and into the open air, and he could only wait to be descended upon and finished off.

Abraham ground his teeth. He would not let it be that easy. He put his foot on the gas pedal and began to drive, leaving his grandfather's home in the rearview mirror.

He had to focus on what was ahead. He had a friend he could go to, a friend who was a surgeon. He could regroup, there.

And yet, he could have sworn he caught sight of Dracula in his mirror—standing on the porch, wreathed in orange flame, and raising a hand to wave.

Abraham blinked and the vampire was gone. He kept driving.

About
The Author

Sirius is a lover of glory, gore, and monsters. They are a queer, nonbinary artist living in the hot and bothered South; currently residing in a little spot that has been dubbed 'Halloweentown', North Carolina. They are the writer of The Draonir Saga, the first book of which is, and The Gentleman Demon Series, the first book of which is *Swallow you Whole*. Sirius began writing at a young age and started exploring the publishing industry when they were thirteen. With many bumps along the way, they have learned a lot and grown in the craft that they would consider their one true love. Queer characters, gothic aesthetics, and royal drama (fantasy of manners) form the foundation of their storytelling. When they are not writing, they work as a professional drag performer, weaving the characters from their stories into visual art for the stage.

MORE BY SIRIUS

The Dread South Series:

Black Jack & Moonshine

THE DEVIL IS GOING TO SET JESSIE FREE.

On a hot Southern morning, Jessie Livingston signed away his soul to a crossroads devil who made him an offer he could not refuse. Now Jessie's voice is dropping, his chest is flattening, and there are hairs sprouting on his chin. He is becoming the man he always wanted to be seen as. Meanwhile, the only thing the devil, Bee, asks for in return is to come collect his due in Jessie's bedroom every Sunday.

Yet, if there is one thing about the devil, it is that he is never satisfied. Bee is determined to push Jessie until he breaks. From Texas to Louisiana in a whirlwind of playing cards, tumbling dice, and flashing casino lights—Jessie finds himself struggling against the snare while falling deeper into iniquity. Yet, when an offer of salvation extends its hand, will he be willing to abandon his only desire to take it?

Funny Little Town

WELCOME TO BUSTAGUT!

Casper's grandmother was the only one who knew that he could see ghosts. Now, she is dead. With her gone, there is nothing to keep him tied down to his family home in Blue Ridge Appalachia. His hope is to start fresh on the beaches of South Florida, but an unexpected detour interrupts his plans for the Sunshine State.

Bustagut is an eerie little carnival town off the beaten path through the mountains. It is run by a shapeshifting clown with very serious ideas of fun, and who loves to play dangerous games with grieving travelers. If Casper can confront his past as well as his fears, he may stand a chance of escaping. Then again, he might just get lost in the endless tricks and traps of this 'funny little town'.

The Gentlemen Demon Series:

Swallow You Whole

HELL IS REAL, AND IT IS HERE

When Violet Clifton sealed her pact with an opportunistic demon, it was her husband's name she signed on the dotted line. Now that his soul has been claimed, she finds herself forming a new deadly alliance. The demon is willing to wear her husband's face, and in compliance with this charade, Violet will not have to remarry. Yet her contract states that she must sign away more souls in order to maintain the bargain. It should be easy enough, as long as she can find more souls to harvest, and she is more than willing to put anyone—including her sickly nephew—on the chopping block.

GOD IS REAL, AND HE THINKS WE'RE SWINE.

Elliot Dosett's fragile health is swiftly declining. His wealthy father wants to send him to a hospital and be rid of him entirely, but Elliot will fight tooth and nail against his fate. In his desperation, he calls out for a demon, only to find that the one who answers may not be entirely what he expected. They strike a bargain for his soul, but the devil fools with best-laid plans when a visit from his aunt Violet turns things sour.

HELL IS CATCHING UP.

Henry and James are two demons who have laid claim to the same soul. Now they are facing an audit from the depths of Hell which could have disastrous effects and upend everything they've worked for. They are willing to plot, scheme, and tempt their way through to the other side, but outsmarting Hell may take more than an act of Satan—it may take an all-out miracle.

Sever Your Spine

James Highmore is a demon who has made a career out of running from Hell. Now he and his companion Henry have found themselves in a world where terror reigns from a bloody throne. It is a realm of decadence, indulgence, and rot. When Henry is threatened by a spine crunching Elder, James discovers exactly how far he will go to save his friend—even if it means enlisting the help of an angel.

Caught between Death's razor teeth, they struggle to survive while dodging Sins, Horsemen, and the very worst of Hell's endless stacks of paperwork.

The Draonir Saga:

Uncrowned

The king is dead.

Long live the king.

Prince Pharun was marked by the gods at birth; yet he has lived his entire life in his younger brother's shadow. Despite becoming Crowned Priest, a right hand to the divine, his father only ever treated him with contempt. Now, the king is dead, and he has named his second son his successor. Pharun is prepared to fight tooth and claw for his birthright, even if that means destroying what little family he has left.

Prince Shrukian has spent his entire life preparing to ascend the throne. When the time comes, he is blindsided by opposition. He never thought that Pharun, the brother he always tried to love, would want to take everything away from him. It hardly seems fair, but Shrukian will not go down without a fight. He will pull on the strings of every foreign and domestic alliance he has, and he is not afraid to challenge the gods.

There is no one to trust in such a perilous game. The one certainty is this; for one king to reign, the other must be uncrowned.

Partitioned

"You will kiss his ring even as he swallows you."

What was once Shrukian's promised birthright is now an uncertain future. In the wake of his brother's threats, he has been forced to flee the capital city and abandon his father's crown. Allies may be hiding in the most unlikely of places, but the price for war is high, and war is what it will take to pry the crown from his brother's claws.

After Shrukian fled, Pharun thought his path to the throne had been cleared. Yet now he is faced with the remnants of the King's Council – men who served under his father and who are willing to stand in his way to preserve the integrity of the throne. The power he wields as the anointed Crowned Priest is not enough. Every painted fan and closed door conceals whispers of intrigue. Before there can be a coronation, heads will have to roll. The greatest uncertainty lies in which one.

Sides are being taken as the crown is passed from hand to hand. In a kingdom rife with subterfuge, even the most loyal hearts and minds will be partitioned.

Condemned

If Pharun was the constant moon...

Then Charlemagne was just a doomed star.

The crown is a heavy burden, and Pharun is still fighting to keep his stolen throne. War with East Avralaen is imminent, but the war to keep peace in his own bedroom is far bloodier. There are those who claim to love him and those who cannot even pretend, and their conspiracies grow thicker by the day.

All Shrukian wants is to return home, but he is moored in Drakkian Province under the Ercole family's watchful tyranny. Specters and madmen plague him at every turn, and he may not survive to take back his rightful throne.

As war looms, Tybalt will stop at nothing to keep those around him safe. The lives of his friends are at stake as everything crumbles around him and the poor are left to perish by a despot king. Dreams of escape fade quickly as he is forced to stay and fight for the lives of those he cares for, as well as his own.

Empires are collapsing. Worlds are being rearranged. Those who do not fight back will surely be captured and condemned.

"I hope that I am the last royal astronomer this palace ever sees."

It is the Age of the Tide. Naiads, an oppressed race of merfolk, are being captured and slaughtered by the score. Queen Robin Brahntaiste has chosen a select few to serve in her court and fill inauspicious roles as astronomers, composers, and sorcerers. Yet, the truth cannot stay buried beneath prestigious titles and opulent clothes. Naiads are not free, and their lives are worth nothing to the cold, arrogant aristocracy.

"As of this writing, there are six of us in the palace. Yesterday, there were seven."

These are the journals and letters of Sopespian Slaine, the Queen's Court High Astronomer and founder of the Red Star Society. Every entry intertwines with a series of eight short stories that offer a glimpse into the intrigue, murder, and dark-hearted motivations that propel the lives of the Society's members.

Horrors, madness, and conspiracies abound. Is there any hope for revolution, or will they all be consumed by Her Majesty's will?

The Red Star Society stands on its own as a bewitching companion to The Draonir Saga.

Hawthorne

SILAS HOLLOW IS A POET.

His work isn't worth much to the elite of Graueyette, such that he has resigned himself to peddling his poems for scraps to earn his living. However, on the heels of defeat arrives a new beginning. A tantalizing offer from a wealthy, mysterious patron promises to change his life.

NICHOLAS SIDOROV IS A DOCTOR.

He is widely renowned as a miracle worker with more gold at his fingertips than even the royal treasury can hold. He claims to be entranced by Silas' words and invites him to stay at Hawthorne as the artist-in-residence. Yet, Nicholas is not what he seems. He remains curiously absent throughout the day, while his lavish home is infested with phantoms as red as the berries of his flowering trees.

Through the doors of Hawthorne Manor, Silas will find himself trapped in the winding halls of a blood-soaked, brightly-lit nightmare set in the world of the Draonir Saga.

3

Favorite Features

Anders

When the portal door slides open on Thursday evening, Gwen is wearing a fitted black skirt that comes to midcalf and a body-hugging black cardigan that accentuates her generous curves. She's wearing cozy shoes, slip-ons that look like cabin slippers. Maybe she forgot to put on regular shoes?

"So what do you think?" she asks, barely inside the workshop. "Will you be able to repair it?"

"I'm afraid not," I say, pushing my digi-mag-specs on top of my head. "Some of the components, including the chip and the retracting gear, are melted."

Soft, pouty lips turn down. "There's nothing you can do?"

She really likes this part, I think, surprised by the spike of jealousy a mechanical cock incites in me. I want to see those gray eyes brighten again.

"I can try to replace the motor," I say, studying the coupling at the base of the penis attachment. "I'm not sure I'll be able to find a compatible one for a model this old. But I am looking."

She blows out a breath. "It's worth a try, isn't it?"

"It'll take time to find one." Not a bad thing, if it keeps her coming around.

"I have every faith you can do it." She rewards me with bright eyes.

"You are an optimist."

"I'm a biochemist living on a space station developing agricultural methods to increase produce for consumption in space and improve food production on Earth. I'd say that requires a certain level of optimism. Wouldn't you agree?" A slight smile curls her lip in sweet punctuation.

It takes me a moment to respond. Not because I need to process her words, but because I want to bask in the sweetness of this woman. Dr. Buttoned-Up-Cardigan is a revelation.

"It does," I say finally. Despite her unfaltering faith, I want her to understand that there's no guarantee I can do this. "If that doesn't work though, we should consider alternative options."

"Of course," she agrees easily. Just like that.

"Even if I do find one, it may take weeks to get to the base."

She leans in, biting her lower lip, and concedes with a hopeful tilt of her chin. "Can we find one on the base?"

"I'm looking," I say, turning my attention to the parts on the table, the silisynth sheath, the inner shell—with silisynth strands braided into a biaxial cylinder, which is stiff but allows for natural flexibility—and the electromechanical core.

"What is it you like about this attachment?" I'm determined to find her a suitable replacement. But I'm also curious.

"Well, this one has a nice soft feel to it. It's fleshy." She slides her finger over the padded swell at the tip, then holds it up for me to touch. I run my finger over the soft mushroom cap. She raises her eyes to me with a sweet smile.

"The newer models have a more realistic texture," I say, trying to stay focused. "They're made with more refined silisynth and rubberized composites."

"Frank-E's also has three sizes," she says, with a hint of stubbornness. "It adjusts, depending on the need. It got stuck in its largest size, but it can also be narrower."

"What are your needs?" I have an idea, but I want to hear her say it. Features like this are useful for anal training. The narrowest setting is almost always used for ass play, although it can also be used to warm up or tease. Several scenarios featuring Gwen play through my mind.

She inhales deeply. Her voice drops an octave as she explains in a professional tone, "I use it for anal penetration." Her face remains serious, but a revealing pink colors her cheeks. The warmth of that blush trickles into my chest and spreads out from there to the rest of my body.

The earnest confession is endearing. Her openness, for someone so buttoned-up, is a turn-on. I keep myself from smiling as I roll the outer sheath over the inner shell that's designed to extend and retract as well as expand and contract.

"Your candid answers are helpful," I tell her, meaning it.

Not wanting to linger on any topic long enough to embarrass her more, I move on. But I don't want her to stop talking. I hand her the shell with the outer coating fitted over it.

"Any other features?" I ask.

She turns the penis attachment over lengthwise in her hands. It's enormous in her delicate hands, although not unrealistically large. I brush off the unexpected giddiness that comes with the sense of relief. I'm not competing with a bot.

"It has different temperatures, hot and cold, in all the sizes," she says, considering the part.

I raise an eyebrow. The function itself isn't surprising, but I'm curious about how she likes to use those features. I almost kick myself for reacting. She'll shut down if she thinks I'm judging or making fun. Or getting turned on. I struggle to maintain my own professionalism.

She interprets my look as doubt. "Oh, yes. The temperature range varies by a lot. It can be set to near freezing or at thermal hot. But that's too much for me."

"How do you use them?"

"Ah ..." The color in her cheeks darkens. "Is that relevant?"

"I guess not." *I just want to know everything about you.* "I'm curious."

I don't play with clients, although on occasion I experiment with the subs from the club or sometimes fellow Doms. That's how I got started tinkering with toys.

"Roxy, project shelves." On the wall behind Gwen, the panels slide open, revealing an array of refurbished sex toys and electrical components.

She slides off the stool with an unselfconscious grace to browse the vibrators and dildos on the shelf behind her. After our conversation so far, I am so hard I can't stand up from behind the bench. While her back is to me, I take the opportunity to adjust myself.

"This is an interesting job," she says as she peruses the assortment.

"I'm not a LovBot, Inc. service technician. I'm more of a hobbyist. But since I'm the only one on the base that knows anything about their products, they ask me to consult for them from time to time. When someone on the base needs a part or a replacement."

I'm also a master Dominant and member at one of the base's intimate pleasures clubs. I keep that detail to myself, not wanting to scare her off.

"Your hobby is tinkering with LovBots?"

I laugh. "And sex toys in general." I meet her gaze. Should I tell her I'm a Dominant? Would she be curious? Would she be wary?

"Oh?" She turns and meets my gaze with analytical gray eyes. "So, you're not a dildo doctor?" Only her slight smile gives away that she's joking.

"I'm a bioelectricmechanical engineer at Katana Corp."

Katana Corp is one of three founding companies of Starbase Lacertas. Space Force, Earth's military machine, owns a third. AgraFirm, the bioagricultural company where Gwen works, owns the other third.

"That's exciting. You're working on the new shuttles?"

The specifics are classified, but Katana is known for its work on the research and recon vessels they've pioneered since they conceived of the station over a century ago.

"No more exciting than a biochemist at AgraFirm." To work there, she'd have to be among the top in her field. Like me.

"I guess." Her answer is breezy, and she returns to studying the collection of sex toys behind her.

"Would you like to take something home to try while I work on the attachment?"

Her gaze shoots to mine, intrigued. "Are you sure?"

"Of course. A loaner." I pick one I think she might like based on what she's told me about her LovBot's irreplaceable pecker. It's a handheld ripple-thruster model. This one has a newer skin coating that's spongier, more natural feeling. "Let me clean it," I say as I drop it into the sterilizer on a nearby shelf.

She smiles wide, and oh my gods, she has dimples. I almost fall to my knees.

When the stericycle completes, I hand it to her wrapped in a stericloth.

"Well, then, I'll wait to hear from you?" she asks, slipping the toy into her shoulder satchel.

I force myself to stop gawking at her and manage to say, "As soon as I have news, I'll contact you."

"It was lovely to see you again. Thank you."

Gwen

I unpack the noodles and veggies I picked up from the market. The flirty engineer working on my LovBot kept running his fingers through his short strawberry-blond hair. It was such a chaotic mess by the time I left, all I wanted to do was finger-comb it into place.

My stomach growls after another late night, but I didn't want to cut our meeting short. I like talking to Dr. Dildo. His energy is easy, judgment-free. Talking about sex must be commonplace in his trade—or hobby.

"Hi, Frank-E," I say as I carry my bowl into the living, but I don't have him initiate. I run my fingers over his neatly styled hair. His stiff synthetic strands don't ruffle under my fingers.

Anders held back his amusement at half the things I said, but his eyes laugh at everything and miss nothing. Do his eyes crinkle like that when he takes a woman? Would he be smiling? Grinning? Scowling?

"Would you like to cuddle with a movie, Gwen?" Frank-E asks as I finish dinner. "There's a sequel to *Ocean World Serpent King* that's become available for viewing."

Anders's toy is burning a hole in my pocket. "That's alright, Frank-E." I leave my bowl in the sink. I'll have Frank-E clean in the morning.

In the shower, I replay our meeting. The way his big brown eyes tracked my gestures. The way those eyes flashed when I explained how I use Frank-E. The way I throbbed when I told him what I like, feeling seen. For the first time in a long time, I imagine someone real—someone other than a vid star from Earth.

I don't bother slipping on panties or a top as I slide into bed, and the soft sheets caress my skin. As I bury myself under thick covers, I imagine what Anders's hands would feel like on my body.

Anders's vibrator is a generous size with a smaller flattened protrusion at its base. It has a remote control with independent buttons for the large shaft and the smaller part. Models like this are usually voice controlled, but the remote is handy if you don't have the commands memorized.

The skin coating is silky yet spongy, reminiscent of real flesh. It's been so long since I touched real skin, I can barely remember how it feels. I bring the tip of the toy to my lips and lick it. The texture is similar to the velvety head of a penis, and it even has a divot at the tip. I wrap my lips around the head. I miss the feeling. My mind conjures Anders's blazing gaze as he orders me to suck, and I give the head a little suck.

I slide my fingers between my legs and find myself lusciously slick. Spreading my legs, I turn on the vibrator mode of Anders's loaner cock and glide it through my folds. I stroke myself with the tip of the large shaft.

The vibrator's pump mechanism allows the shaft to extend and retract, thrusting up and down instead of simply vibrating. The smaller vibrating protrusion can be pressed against the clit or the backhole for external stimulation while the shaft remains inserted.

I set the vibrator on low and glide it up and down over my pussy, imagining Anders demonstrating how to use it. I use the remote to increase the speed as I circle my clit. My body thrums, and I ease back into my pillows, allowing the soft vibration to warm me up.

When I'm ready to slide Anders's toy inside, I tease myself with it. I insert it an inch at first, pulling in and out, giving myself more with each push. I imagine

Anders being gentle with me, fucking me slowly, making sure I can take all of him. At first.

When it's seated all the way inside me, I press the flat protrusion against my clit and press the thrust button on the remote. The thick shaft begins pumping into me while the smaller vibrator hums against my clit, and I'm immediately lost to the dual sensation. Vibration and slippery friction. All my blood flow is rerouted to my swollen cunt.

Climbing toward my climax is gradual, my thoughts lingering on all the ways Anders would touch me. I force myself to settle and relax into the sensations arresting my awareness until at last the coil tightening in my core snaps. I succumb to a splendorous release as wave after sumptuous wave rolls through my body.

I reach over and drop the toy onto a towel ready on my nightstand. As my body wallows in the decadent release, I wrap my arms around one of my larger pillows and drift off to sleep with visions of a sexy, commanding technician wrapping himself around me.

The next morning over a breakfast of boiled eggs and cut fruit, Frank-E plays a message Anders left after I'd gone to bed. He looked at my part and wants to talk about it. I agree to meet him at his workshop after work on Monday. It gives me the weekend to enjoy his toy and dream of all the things he could do to me with it.

4

Repairing the Phallus Part

Anders

Gwen is at my workshop at 7:00 p.m. sharp. She's wearing a loose-fitting dark-gray dress that hits just below her knees and a cotton cardigan that hangs off her body like a sack. She's breathtaking.

Her hair is in a high bun again. The overwhelming urge to pull out the two ornate pins holding it in place and let it spill over her shoulders is compelling, but I resist.

"Come in," I say, directing her to sit on a stool at my work bench. "Would you like something to drink?"

"I'm fine, thank you. How did you make out?" she asks, getting straight to the point. "Are you able to fix the phallus?"

I try not to smile at her word choice. "Sadly, I won't be able to replace the motor."

Her shoulders slump and the expectant vibrance on her face dims, casting a shadow over my very existence.

"But," I add quickly, "maybe I can retrofit an attachment from a newer model. The problem with your LovBot ..."

"Frank-E."

"Yes, Frank-E. The problem is that the components in both the motor and the electrical chip are melted so the neural processor can't communicate with the phallus." I ramble, not wanting to lose the striking gaze she has fixed on me.

Gwen listens with her whole body, leaning toward me, her elbows on the table, her wide eyes taking in every word. She's poised like a cat, a tiger, alert to her surroundings. She's no shy kitten. She's just drawn in, watching.

She smiles and light fills the room.

"It's going to take time for me to find a part that I can retrofit," I say, unable to take my eyes off hers. "But be prepared in case I can't."

Her light dims again.

"I propose we look at alternatives."

She perks up, intrigue written all over her face. I'm helpless to the sway her expressions have over my mood.

"Let's compare attachments of other LovBot models. Maybe I can retrofit the parts to your ... uh ... Frank-E."

"Would that be possible?"

"Consumers have been lamenting that manufacturers don't make product attachments universal for centuries. Companies make more money forcing you to purchase whole new units. It will be a challenge to find something compatible."

"Do you think you can do it?"

"No, but with your optimism, why not try?"

Her eyes snap to mine, and a soft blush paints her cheeks. My inquisitive tiger likes to be seen.

"Let's look at some newer models," I continue, "and see what the options are."

"But you'll look for a replacement motor in the meantime?"

"If there's one out there, I'll find it. I've already started a search and reached out to my contact at LovBot, Inc. But you should look for a new bot." Then

I add, wanting her to understand, "Not that I'm not enjoying our regular meetings."

She bites her lip and her flush deepens.

"Let's see what features the other bots have. Then we can take notes on any models that pique your interest."

She opens her mouth to protest, but I give her a stern look to stave off her objection. "Just in case. For backup."

She drops her chin and peers up through eyelashes with a look that has my very real cock standing at attention. If she weren't so earnest, I'd think she was practiced, but that look is pure instinct. A gesture that's both submissive and seductive.

"Okay," she says, acquiescing sweetly to my silent command. *Definitely submissive.*

"That's my good scientist."

She smiles, flashing dimples. My tiger also likes to be praised.

Gwen

His words are a heat-seeking missile that detonates between my legs. He holds out his hand, palm up. I look at it for a moment. I'm being persnickety, but I like my bot. He's familiar. Comfortable. Predictable.

I almost laugh out loud at the thought of a LovBot being anything but predictable, but I stop myself just in time. Anders is placating but patient as usual. He must think I'm unbalanced with my attachment to a robotic sex toy. Maybe I am, but I like what I like.

His smile is open and engaging. The type of man who's an open book. But sometimes we don't know we're keeping secrets. My ex didn't know. Sometimes our secrets are simply who we are. We're not always transparent. Even to ourselves.

My ex didn't know that hurting me would make him feel good when we started experimenting, and he struggled with that side of himself. Until we realized I would never satisfy the secret part of himself that he had been unaware of. Until I woke that hunger.

My arrangement with Anders is business. How deep do I need to see into who he is? I rest my hand in his big one, which is warm to the touch. When his fingers wrap around mine, the touch is reassuring. I can't help but stroke his hand with my thumb, noticing the soft-yet-rough texture of real skin. I glance at him. His smile is gone, replaced by an intensity that could pull me in if I let it.

"Let's sit over here. It's a little more comfortable." He leads me to a well-loved armchair in a cozy corner of his workshop.

He pulls a crate beside the chair and squats on it so we're at eye level.

"Roxy, open holovid."

The screen appears in front of us. An antiquated brass retractable-arm wall sconce reminiscent of the technaissance era that began in the late 1900s is mounted over the chair.

"I did a search for the specs you described and narrowed it down to a few models. Let's take a look?"

"Yes," I say, unable to hide my curiosity. He's taken all the legwork out of searching for a new bot.

His smile is wide, rewarding me with all his happy wrinkles.

"Our first candidate is Fabian-D."

"Fabian?"

"Yeah. He looks like he could be a super spy."

"Not my type at all."

"What is your type?"

"Frank-E," I say without thinking.

"I'll have to meet Frank-E. What's he like?"

"Quiet. Unassuming. Reliable. There are no surprises with Frank-E."

The crinkles around Anders's eyes and mouth double in number, making me feel like I've revealed too much. He sees straight into me, but he lets my comment slide without prying.

"Okay. Let's look at Fabian-D. You may not like the bot, but his features might interest you. Roxy, show partlist."

The holovid displays a list of Fabian-D's bot parts.

"Roxy, penis options and specifications, please."

The screen zooms in on detailed features with image icons.

"Roxy, show us the thrust options."

Memories of Anders's toy flood my mind as the picture of an olive-toned silisynth cock appears on the vid. A memory of the way Anders's loaner cock moved smoothly inside me makes me shift in my seat. I look at him. He's watching the screen. His profile is defined with a strong, clean-shaven chin. He'd had late afternoon scruff on our first meeting. Did he shave after work? I want to reach out and stroke his cheek. He turns his head toward me for confirmation. I look away quickly, but not before I catch his lip quirk.

"That's nice," I say, trying to maintain some strain of professionalism. "What does it say about its sizes?"

"It only has the one."

"Oh." I can't keep the disappointment out of my voice.

"But he has dexterous fingers, and you could always complement with other toys. Or people."

"Well, yes, if we're considering Fabian as a replacement bot, but not if we're looking at retrofitting his penis for Frank-E."

When I look back at Anders, he's studying me. His eyes are so penetrating I lose my train of thought.

"Okay, not Fabian," he says. "Let's put him on the backup list."

"I'm not sure," I say dubiously.

His smile returns. "His cock changes temperatures too."

I feel heat rise on my face, and it's like his smile lines wink at me. He's making fun, but it doesn't bother me. The kindness in his eyes makes it okay. This is flirting. *He's flirting with me.* It's been so long I almost didn't recognize it. Sometimes a bold intern will flirt with me, but I don't encourage them.

I can't help the smile that creeps onto my face as awareness tingles on my skin.

"What about his texture? Is he soft?"

"Like Frank-E?"

"No, like yours."

His eyes widen.

"I mean, the one you loaned me." I must be radiating heat now, and I resist the urge to put my cool hands to my face.

"Ah." His smile broadens. He looks at the screen. "It's made of the same coating composite, so it would be as soft."

"Okay. Maybe the short list then," I say.

We go through a few more candidates, but none are Frank-E. These bots are all flashy and dynamic, big muscles and rugged physiques. As tall and broad-shouldered as Anders, although I can't imagine he's as toned under his clothes as these models are crafted to appear.

A loud rumble escapes my stomach at that moment. A frown steals Anders's playful smile, but it returns almost as quick as it disappeared, twice as bright.

"Would you like something to eat? I can whip up some dinner."

"No, thank you," I say, looking at the time. "It's late. Thank you for taking the time to help me."

"Not at all. This has been fun."

Of course, it had been. He made me blush at regular intervals. He's probably making a game of it.

"I'd like to see Frank-E. I want to know what makes the bot so special."

I laugh. "Okay. How about Sunday afternoon?"

"Maybe I can build something for you to your preferred specifications."

"You could do that?"

"I could try. Let's talk about it Sunday."

5

Subspace Entanglements

Anders

I slide my identlet over the door sensor next to the coat room.

"Welcome, Dr. Nevis. Have a nice evening."

"Thank you, Justine."

I descend the sweeping staircase to the lower gallery and make my way to Subspace's bar and lounge at the center. The first floor is a marketplace of sex-related amusements and merchandising. Scene rooms and shops line the gallery beneath the second-story balcony. The Satellite, a smaller and more intimate bar, occupies one end of the gallery. The floor is dotted with small exhibition spaces featuring live performances and demonstrations, lounge seating areas, and kiosks providing toy sanitizing services or peddling toys and props. The second floor, the mezzanine level where the club's entrance is located, leads to private rooms and apartments.

I scan the bar seating, and Malcolm raises his tumbler to catch my attention. I make my way to meet the club owner at his preferred seat, nodding to friends and other members. Clarise, a server, intercepts me and takes my order before I reach Malcolm.

Across the gallery, we have a view of two men strapping a woman to a spanking bench set up on a dais. She's wearing a sheer babydoll with no panties. The table is tilted so her ass is pointed upward, and her legs are parted so she's exposed to the room. I've worked with her before. She's popular because she's responsive, and she loves an audience.

Malcolm starts in before I've taken a seat. "What has you so occupied these days? I haven't seen you in weeks."

"A project. It's kind of tricky. I have a client who wants a replacement for an old bot model."

"Why so tricky?"

"I won't be able to fix it, but she's really attached to her bot."

Malcolm laughs. "So it's the client that's tricky, not the project."

"Pretty much." I sip my drink and scan the periphery of the room. It's early on a weeknight, so the atmosphere is relaxed.

"Just tell the client you won't be able to fix it."

"Then she won't come back."

Malcolm's eyes narrow at me. "So ask her out."

I glance at the trio at the spanking bench. The two men—regulars—stand back, engrossed in conversation. They're probably discussing climate control, their objective to build the sub's anticipation.

A woman approaches the table. Giselle, the woman who stole Malcolm's heart, joins us. She's wearing a short, silky robe that's pale and nearly transparent. Malcolm, in his normal black slacks, black tunic, and collarless black suit jacket, extends his arm to her. She nestles into his side on the sofa, and he hands her the drink he has ready for her.

I never thought Malcolm would attach himself to one woman, but you can never predict when you'll meet your person. Giselle is sweet and gentle. Malcolm's perfect complement, her silly to his serious, her fire to his ice, her unstoppable to his immovable. The man is completely absorbed in her.

I didn't think I was ready to meet my person, but now that I can't get a certain scientist out of my mind, I'm open to the possibility. Do I believe she's the one? No idea. But I'd like to find out why she has my conduits seizing.

After Giselle greets me, Malcolm pulls her into our conversation. "Anders was just explaining about a client that's sizzling his wires and why he can't ask her out."

"Really?" Giselle asks with a wry smile.

I haven't known Giselle long, but she feels like an old friend.

"That's the tricky part. I'm repairing her toy."

"And you don't want her to feel like you're creeping on her," Giselle says, astute as ever.

"Yeah. She's also attached to her bot, and I don't want to be the one to tell her it's ready for the recycler, let her down. She won't be happy when I finally tell her I can't fix it. I'm trying to get her to look at other bot models."

"Or human models?" Giselle's grin is coy, and Malcolm laughs.

"Or human," I agree.

"So what's the trouble?"

"I don't want to come at her too hard and scare her off. Seem like I'm taking advantage of her pleasurebot-lessness."

"You're buying time to get to know her."

"Exactly."

"Why don't you bring her here?" Malcolm asks.

"He doesn't know her well enough," Giselle answers for me. "You wouldn't want this to be your first date if you're still getting to know her. Not unless you know this is her scene. And if she's attached to her bot, she may not be a people-oriented person. This *is* tricky. And this might be the last place she'd want to be."

"Ask her out," Malcolm says. "You don't have to bring her here. But ask soon or it will be creepier later."

"I can't get a read on her. She's not shy, but she's reserved. Not hiding, necessarily, but she's content with her bot at home. I don't know what her story is. I can't find out more without asking."

"Submissive?" Malcolm asks.

"Yeah. She's got submissive tendencies, but I can't tell if she knows that about herself. She's guarded."

"Well, bring her here. Reserve a suite. You don't have to start with a scene room."

At the spanking bench, the taller of the two men begins snapping leather straps in the air, making a show of testing the impact-play instruments. From this angle, the sub's pussy is glistening in the light. So ready. Knowing her, the spanking will push her over the edge. These masters are skilled.

"I'd like to start with dinner. Not a sex club."

"Then what are you waiting for?" Malcolm asks.

Giselle says, "He's waiting until he finishes the project. Have her get to know him. So she doesn't see him as a creeper that works on vibrators in his spare time."

I open my mouth, but Malcolm cuts me off. "He's not a creep."

I chuckle at him defending me.

"She doesn't know him well enough to judge that yet," Giselle responds.

"Yeah, but—" I try to interject.

"He's more than a dildo repairman," Malcolm insists.

"I am." I manage to break into their debate. "I'd like her to see that before ..."

"Okay," Malcolm says, leaning forward with his forearms on his thighs. "Once you've finished, however it turns out, ask her out. Either you can celebrate your success, or you can lament the failure of the project together."

Giselle sips her drink before adding, "I think that might be best. In the meantime, get to know each other."

Malcolm leans back in his seat and crosses his arms, studying me.

Giselle side-eyes him. "I recognize that look."

"Me too," I say, "and I don't like it."

Malcolm tends to dominate over everyone, not just his subs. I ready myself for gospel.

He scans the room slowly before turning back to me. "While I'm enjoying your starstruck-where-the-fuck-am-I state, I'm going to miss watching you work the room. I never thought I'd see a day when you'd forgo sampling the banquet feast to settle in for a simple meal at home. I'm looking forward to meeting the woman who's humbling you."

Malcolm has been an enthusiastic co-pilot in my journey from fledgling lothario to master-level Dominant and aficionado of the art of intimate play. For most of my adult life, I've enjoyed tangle-free engagements. Now, having witnessed the range of emotions play over Gwen's expressive face, I'm captive to the idea of entanglement with her.

We watch the stage as one of the Doms delivers artful blows to the sub's ass and thighs with a soft leather crop. The other, the more experienced Dom, offers suggestions. The sub arches her back and strains against her leg straps to meet the blows. Her glistening folds are on display for all to see.

Malcolm leans over and whispers in Giselle's ear. She turns to watch the trio.

"Ask her out soon," Malcolm tells me as he takes Giselle's hand and rests it on his thigh in a possessive grip. "I don't want you to miss your opportunity for something great."

The Dom wielding the crop drops it and gets on his knees behind the sub. As she bucks in her straps, trying to grind into the bench, he holds her thighs firmly and begins licking at her pussy.

We linger over our drinks a while longer before Malcolm sets his empty tumbler on the coffee table in front of him.

"I'm glad we could get you to come out for a while." Catching Giselle's gaze, he says, "Giselle and I are going up to my suites. Do you want to join us?"

Just weeks ago, I'd have enjoyed helping my friend take his own something great to the next level of pleasure, but now the idea doesn't carry the same appeal as tracking down my own tiger.

"Not tonight," I say, setting my own glass on the table.

Malcolm smirks. "She's got you all tied up, hasn't she."

"Let's just say she's got me curious."

Giselle gives me a knowing wink. "You're heading home?"

"I am indeed."

"Don't wait too long," Malcolm says as they accompany me to the sweeping staircase that leads to the mezzanine. "Ask her soon."

"I plan to."

6

Measuring the Value of a LovBot

Anders

Sunday afternoon can't come fast enough. Asking Gwen out on a date when her personal pleasure device fails feels opportunistic, maybe predatory, but Malcolm and Giselle's advice to ask her out sooner than later plays in my mind. I'll ask her tonight.

I arrive at Gwen's apartment ready to meet the quiet-and-unassuming Frank-E, curious about the staying power of *le* LovBot. She comes to the door wearing fitted black workout shorts and a thin, fitted t-shirt topped with another cotton cardigan. This one is a vibrant Day-Glo green. Seeing her out of her somber professional colors is a pleasant surprise. Her hair is tied back in a loose ponytail, and her long, dark waves are pulled forward over one shoulder.

I feel a little overdressed in slacks and a collarless tunic. Gwen's relaxed loungewear—inadvertently sexy as it is—is a splash of cold water. This is not a date. Leave it to my little tiger to be unambiguous. Her directness is that much sexier.

Her apartment is a vibrant splash of color and plush furnishings. My buttoned-up tiger shines bright in the fluorescent cardigan. The whimsy suits her.

She leads me to the living where the serene-looking, sandy-haired LovBot is seated on the couch.

"This is Frank-E," she says.

"Hey, Frank-E. How's it hanging?" I say, and she laughs, her dimples making an appearance.

If I thought her smile brightened a room, her laugh is a supernova that obliterates any traces of darkness in my soul. I add making this woman laugh—and often—to my list of life goals.

Frank-E turns his head to face me and the sides of his mouth tilt upward. "It's not currently hanging. It has been removed. And you, Doctor?"

She laughs again. "That's as close to self-aware as Frank-E gets."

"I'm fine, Frank-E," I answer the bot.

Still chuckling, she says, "Frank-E, take off your robe please."

I'm relieved she treats her LovBot like the appliance that he is. Her personal attachment is of the standard variety and doesn't enter the realm of obsessive.

He removes his robe in a smooth motion, not jerky like some older models. When she said she'd gotten it secondhand, I worried he might be some ancient artifact or a family heirloom. More realistic domestic multi-functional bots, including sexbots, have shorter lifespans than bots with dedicated functionality. This bot is around a decade old and appears to be well-maintained.

He stands with a flat coupling ring where his penis should be. A castrated male with a metal-and-silicone machine base where his dick should be would make the most enlightened man's balls crawl up inside him. I'm not immune, and I sympathize with Frank-E.

The bot is tall. I like that his stomach, while flat, doesn't have an unrealistic excess of muscles. All the LovBots I researched for Gwen were modeled after hyper-toned bodybuilders or surfers. I mean, I work out, but I think they add extra muscles to some of those bots.

"What do you think?" she asks, worrying the hem of her oversized cardigan.

"He's exactly as you described. Quiet and unassuming."

She laughs again, releasing her grip on her covering. Throwing her hands up in a show of full disclosure, she says, "No secrets here." She is an open book, her expressive face telling me all her stories, thoughts, and desires.

A twinge of guilt runs through me. I wouldn't drag out the repair process with anyone else. I shouldn't have committed to trying to fix the part.

"Would you like something to drink? I have wine, beer, juice, and water. I also have snacks."

She sweeps her hand, gesturing for me to sit anywhere, more at ease in her own space than she'd been in my workshop.

She leaves the room and returns with a platter of cheeses and sliced fruit. "I'm afraid this is all I know how to cook. And coffee or tea. I can cook those."

"It's perfect."

When we sit, Gwen gets right to the point. "What do you need to design me my own pleasure part?"

"It would help if you told me how you use your LovBot. What are the features you use most?"

She looks over to the bot and bites her lip, considering. "So many ways," she mumbles under her breath. "I'd almost have to demonstrate."

Her voice is so soft I almost miss her words.

"I'm sorry," I say. "What?"

She turns to me, and her face brightens with a shaky laugh. The speculative gaze she was giving the bot shifts to something different as her face flushes. The nibble to her lip reveals a different type of speculation.

"It's up to you," I prompt, tentatively.

There's heat in her eyes. The air between us pulses.

"If you want to show me ..." Lost in her eyes, the words trip out of my mouth before I realize I've spoken aloud, and they trail off.

She's intrigued. If I were to order her now, she would comply. I see it in the way she leans toward me, hanging on my words. There's tension in her shoulders. She wants to be told what to do. But I need her to tell me.

"You'd want to watch?" She bites her lower lip.

Fuck. Decelerate your revolutions, I tell myself. *You want her to get to know you.* The temperature in the room spikes. But her smile, now marred by concerned lines in her furrowed brow, short-circuits all my wiring.

In the club, subs' goals and motivations are out in the open. New members are accompanied by veterans and established members. Their dress, their interactions with other members, and their participation in the scene rooms are all out in the open. Dominants receive training at the club before they can adopt the title, and they know what questions to ask before initiating play. Once new members pass the introductory phase of club initiation, all members—Doms, subs, switches; every Subspace member and employee—should know proper club etiquette. The rules are strict, but that's to ensure the safety of all members. Doms—experienced ones, at any rate—are prepared to navigate sensitive situations.

None of those rules apply with clients outside the club looking to repair toys that they use alone. In a rush, I realize I haven't met a woman outside the controlled parameters of the club in years. Even those who seek my expertise, I meet at the club. Gwen's description of Frank-E as predictable makes sense.

Now Gwen is stepping out of her comfort zone. The trust she shows me knocks me off balance.

"Yes," I answer. "I want to watch. But only if you're comfortable with that."

"Seriously?" She scoots forward to the edge of the sofa. "I mean, I'm no prude, obviously. I've come to you about my sex toys, and you are a sex toy expert." Her skin flushes that pretty pink I love.

Is she considering this? In that case, yes, I'm serious. Dead. Fucking. Serious. I want to see what the flush looks like under her clothes. *Fuck.* I want her naked. Except for that cardigan. She should keep the cardigan on.

"It takes me a long time. You'll be bored."

A laugh escapes before I can stop it, but when I see her bite her lip, I realize she's serious. She clears her throat. She's embarrassed about how long it takes her to cum. Had some fucker criticized her, not given her the time she needed to enjoy herself? I school the scowl that threatens when I try to puzzle out why she prefers intimacy with a robot. I keep my expression soft, not wanting her to feel ridiculed by me. I don't know her story, but I intend to find out.

"This isn't about me." I mean it. As much as I want this—want her—I want her to feel safe around me. "It's about seeing what works for you. What you like."

She scoots forward to the edge of the sofa cushion and leans toward me. Her voice is almost a whisper. "I don't think I'm wet." It's an admission.

I doubt that, based on the dilated irises engulfing the gray of her eyes, the exaggerated pulse in her throat, and the way she licks her lips.

"Make yourself wet. Show me what you like," I encourage.

She keeps to herself for a reason. If I push, she'll retreat. Instead of strategizing any moves, I need to follow her lead and simply be here for her.

Gwen

Do I want to masturbate for my own personal vibrator designer, the dildo doctor? Yes, in all my fantasies, more than anything I've ever wanted in my life. I shocked myself when the words spilled out of my mouth, but now that they're out, there's no calling them back. And if the beads of sweat breaking out on his forehead are any indication, he is interested.

"What exactly would you be looking for?" I ask, holding back from embarrassing myself by climbing into his lap.

"How you use your toys. The way you use the features. How fast or slow you like the settings." He sips his drink, and my gaze drops to where his throat bobs as he swallows. "Where you use them."

His deep, compelling voice ripples through me, and I want to show him everything. I savor the way his eyes study my face, my mouth, my eyes. I want his eyes to drop and study the rest of me. Goose pimples rise on my skin.

He's been sweet. Patient. Encouraging. And he's so beautiful. He commands with soft words and arresting eyes. My fantasies of Anders surge to the surface, all reasonable thoughts erased. It's been so long since I've been with a man.

How do I do this? The words are poised on my lips to answer him. To tell him what I want. But a little voice creeps up, reminding me to slow down. How do I tell him what I want without coming off as a sex-starved, depraved, fuckbot-dependent recluse? How do I ask without repelling him? I guess it doesn't matter. Once he's built my custom sex toy, he'll move on.

His hands flex and clench in his lap. They're big, and his fingers are long. I recall the dexterous way they manipulate his tools.

"I'll keep my hands to myself." His words bring me back to my senses.

"Yes. No touching. Strictly professional. Of course." I force a small smile and try not to show my disappointment. This is professional for him. But the thought of performing for him overshadows the disappointment. I almost change my mind, but he smiles.

"Professional," he says, though he's flushed. Maybe he's as affected as I am?

He'll keep his hands to himself. Sex with a near-stranger doesn't get more innocuous than hands-free, except he doesn't feel like a stranger. The thought of his hands on me doesn't scare me. There's no doubt his hands would be as gentle or as rough as I'd want them to be.

In all the years I'd been with my ex, I'd never predicted his need to inflict pain. After mere weeks of knowing Anders, I'm sure he'd never hurt me—not in a way that I didn't enjoy. I can't explain my certainty.

He's on the edge of his seat on the armchair, leaning forward. Our knees are almost touching.

"What do you want me to use?" I ask. Though my heart is racing, I'm relaxed by his presence.

His response is quick. "The toy I lent you. Have you used it?"

"Yes." My voice comes out breathy. *I used it while I thought of you*, I don't say.

"Show me."

Without another word, I'm up and striding with purpose to my sleep chamber. I'd run, but my last fibers of decency have me showing a bit of self-restraint. I have nothing to lose. Why not live out a fantasy while I can?

When I come back with the toy and a towel, he's dragged the ottoman in front of the couch and is perched on it.

"Take off your pants."

His commanding tone infuses my core with an addictive heat. I don't know what it is about Anders's voice, but I want to ask permission to take the rest of my clothes off too. I envision myself kneeling before him. He makes me wish I was a bot he could command freely to serve him. Does he have a LovBot of his own?

My t-shirt falls just below my unshaved mound. I'm not sure I could be less sexy if I tried. I didn't dress up for our visit because I didn't want to make more out of it than a simple business-quarters call. I regret that now.

My hands go to the hem of my shirt, but he stops me with a shake of his head. Okay, he's going to focus on my crotch. I can respect that.

"Take your shirt off but put the cardigan back on."

"Okay." Curious, I do as he instructs.

When my lime-green cardigan is back on, I pull the panels together in the front. He stops me again.

"Let it fall open."

I pull the panels open, sliding them over my sensitive nipples. The side panels frame my breasts, my stomach, my hips, and the tuft of hair between my legs. His chest expands broadly as he takes in an enormous breath, then his shoulders settle as he lets the air out slowly. The tingling on my skin ratchets up a degree, and I shiver under his gaze.

"Good," he says, his warm smile showing his pleasure. "Sit back on the couch."

He gestures to the center seat of the couch, facing where he sits on the ottoman.

I spread the towel out on the cushions. When I sit, he commands, "Knees up."

His words resonate low inside me. Again, they target the part of my body open and exposed to him. I comply, my gaze locked on his. It's like a game of Anders Says. The only bit of control I have here is the power to move slowly, which I leverage to maximum effect. I slide my heels up and brace them against the edge of the cushion, spacing them wide to give him the view he wants.

He wipes a hand over his face.

I slide my fingers over my folds and spread my lips to reveal myself to him. I'm slick. I spread my moisture around and up to my clit.

The tip of his tongue moistens his lower lip. "I knew you'd be wet for me." His voice is a low groan as he raises his gaze to meet mine.

Without breaking eye contact, I use the remote to switch the vibrator on the small appendage on at its lowest setting. Anders blows out a breath when I spread my folds open with one hand. I touch the vibrator to my clit, and we both groan.

His glance shifts to my pussy. I slide the low-humming vibrator over my clit and rock against it before gliding it down to the entrance of my channel and back up. I spread my liquid heat, enjoying the soft purr of the toy against my tender flesh.

"Watch me," I whisper. This may be the most aroused I've ever been.

His gaze flashes to mine before returning to the vibrator at work. He holds his hand out to where I hold the remote. I put it in his hand, allowing my fingers to brush his palm. He shudders slightly. He likes this, and that knowledge empowers me. I spread my legs wider and slide my ass closer to the edge of the cushion. He rewards me with a groan that's like a caress.

I get wetter as I slide the vibrator over my clit and down to the entrance of my channel. He licks his lips and increases the vibration speed with the remote. I moan in response.

With his eyes on mine, it won't take me long to cum.

"Slide it in," he orders.

He means the longer appendage. I do as he says. I let my head fall back, but don't take my eyes off him as the thick length glides against my inner walls. I pull it out a little, and then dip it in farther, teasing, taking my time, deepening the thrust each time.

The breath he lets out slices through the tension between us. "Fuck yourself with it."

I tilt my hips forward and plunge the toy in. His eyes on my pussy make the sensations so much more intense.

"Turn it around."

Without question, I pull the toy out enough to twist it, the smaller appendage now nestled against my asshole. The vibration sends tingles through to my core, and my walls clench around the shaft. I leave the shaft inserted, not fucking myself with it, but enjoying the sensation of the smaller part against my rosebud.

Then the speed of the smaller part increases to its highest setting, and my need revs up like he's controlling me with the remote.

"Don't move it away," he orders.

"Yes, sir," I whisper, meeting his gaze. The heat there melts me, and when the cock begins to extend and retract inside me, I can't look away from Anders's face. Engaging the thrust feature, he's fucking me remotely. He's not watching my cunt spread wide and impaled with an electric phallus. He's locked in on my face.

"Work your clit," he says.

I do, using my fingers to spread more moisture from my entrance to my clit. I am on the cusp, the muscles in my lower belly and core tightening. The growing tension has me gasping.

Anders shifts to sit next to me in a smooth, catlike movement. There's barely a breath of space between us as he drapes one arm across the couch behind me and rests his other hand on his knee.

"Cum for me," he whispers, his breath caressing my ear.

He watches my face as the toy thrusts over and over. My hips rock as the shaft pumps until finally the rhythm grips me and I'm swept away. I drop my head back against the couch, succumbing to the sensation. My pussy spasms around the toy with an orgasm explosive enough to spray my hands. I close my eyes, sensing his eyes on me, basking in his presence as waves of pleasure ripple through me.

"That's the most beautiful thing I've ever seen." His voice is low and soft against my ear.

Anders

Spread out before me is the luscious sight of a satisfied tiger. The glow of satiation eclipses the traces of doubt that live in her eyes. Someday, it will be me lavishing her with toe-curling pleasure. Right now, she needs to feel safe with me, to keep that ever-pervasive doubt at bay.

If she says no touching, she should be able to trust that. I won't touch her until I know she's ready. Someday, she'll beg me to touch her, and she'll know my touch is worship.

With my arm draped across the back of the sofa, I loom over her. Looking up into my face with pleading eyes, she reaches out with her cum-coated hand to grip my tunic. My cock jumps to attention.

"Your pace."

She doesn't extract the full shaft but slides it out enough to pull the vibration away from her ass. I turn off the minor appendage and slow the thrust mechanism to its lowest setting.

"I want to watch you fuck Frank-E," I tell her.

She gasps, but it's not shock or offense I see in her face. She likes this, me telling her what to do.

Her surprise morphs into laughter. "He doesn't have a penis."

"I brought it." Then to Frank-E, I say, "Frank-E, sit on the couch."

"Yes, sir," Frank-E answers and moves to sit on the couch on the other side of Gwen.

I extract myself from my seat, careful not to touch her, but close enough that I smell her light floral scent, salty sweat, and heady arousal. She releases her grip on my tunic, and I mourn the lost connection with her. I retrieve Frank-E's part, wrapped in a stericloth, from my satchel and then return to reattach his penis.

"Is it safe?"

"I took out the internal mechanisms, and I replaced the shell. The soft coating is intact."

Fortunately, the part was set at its maximum girth when it blew, so my tiger will be filled tight.

"Straddle him facing me. I want to watch you cum."

She watches me with those pensive eyes as she moves with long, languid movements like a tiger. Stalking her prey, her eyes never leave mine, holding me captive, as she swings her leg over Frank-E's lap. My tiger in motion. Breathtaking. I've never been happier to be hunted.

The sight gives me the urge to take her to visit a Siberian wildlife preserve on Earth.

Gwen

Anders slides the ottoman sideways to sit in front of Frank-E as I straddle the bot. He watches my face as I lean forward to position Frank-E's appendage at my entrance, bracing my hands on the bot's knees.

The silisynth cock is at its largest girth, and though I'm slick, I have to work myself slowly onto it. Anders eyes drop from my face to watch me take the cock, and I lean back to give him a better view. His throat bobs up and down as he swallows.

Having his undivided attention sends a flush of tingling warmth through my body as I feel the rigid phallus stroke my inner walls in short, gentle thrusts. I close my eyes as I ride the attachment slowly, each time I sink onto it taking it deeper.

"That's it. Ride that shaft. Let it fill your cunt. Does that feel good?"

His blunt words, his throaty coaxing, pour over me like a caress.

I lick my lips. "Yes." I push down a little more.

I lower all the way down, seating myself completely on the cock.

"Look at me," he orders in a tone that ripples over me.

I open my eyes to Anders's approving smile.

Frank-E's sensors register my recorded patterns, and anticipating my need for thrust, he grips my hips with hard mechanical hands. Normally, he would engage the thrust-retract feature of his phallus, but lacking the ability to engage, he grips my hips and leans back preparing to buck into me with his body.

"Sit back, Frank-E," Anders says. "Gwen is going to ride you."

Frank-E releases his grip on my hips.

"So sexy." Anders raises both his hands and extends them toward my shoulders. "May I?"

My head bobs up and down. I don't know what I'm agreeing to, and I don't care. He can do anything he wants to me.

He pushes my cardigan off my shoulders, fingers brushing my skin, and the light covering drops to my elbows. It binds my arms to my sides loosely as it frames my breasts for his view.

"Ride him. Let me watch you take that cock."

I do, slow at first. The stroking against my inner walls quickly fills me with the need to move faster. I slide forward then drop back, feeling the fullness over and over.

I usually need more time, especially after cumming once, but his eyes on me and his coaxing words are all the added stimulation I need.

"Such a needy pussy. I bet you work your toys hard."

At his words, my muscles clench around the attachment. I know it won't take much longer. I shudder.

"Touch your clit. Make yourself cum for me."

The angle of the penis allows me to push back and forth easily. I lean forward and brace myself on Frank-E's knees with one hand as I slide my other back to rub my clit.

"That's it. Fuck yourself harder."

I reach out and grip Anders's tunic, clutching it tight and using the solid wall of his chest to propel myself back and forth as I slam down on Frank-E. I arch my back, giving Anders a clear view of my breasts bouncing. I feel my face contort as I chase my orgasm with Anders's encouragement. At last, the first cascade of release washes over me, followed by wave after wave of muscle-spasming ecstasy. I fall forward to rest my head against Anders's shoulder. He scoots forward, taking my weight against his warm body.

"Such a good girl. So beautiful. I'll never forget how beautiful you look cumming for me like that. You're a work of art."

I shudder as I slide up and down a few times on Frank-E's inert shaft, both fists gripping Anders's shirt. He grips my upper arms to support me, but the touch is tentative. I want him to wrap his arms around me, but I don't ask.

He breathes heavy into my hair as though we'd just competed to see who'd cum first.

"Slide off," he whispers. "I'm going to hold you now. Is that okay?"

I roll my head up and down against him in an awkward and emphatic yes, wanting so badly to feel him against me. I lift myself, dislodging Frank-E, and Anders pulls my cardigan up onto my shoulders. He brings the front panels together in front of me, then gathers me against him and pulls me onto his lap.

He stands with me in his arms and, after some maneuvering, sits on the couch with his legs up on the cushions. He leans against the armrest with me nestled between his legs, my side pressed against his front. His arms wrap around me, cocooning me in the warmth of his embrace.

A warm breath fans over me as he sighs against my hair. "So sweet. I don't think I'll be able to let go."

My legs are pulled up so my knees are draped over his thigh. I can't speak, lost in the sumptuous feel of his body pressed against mine and his firm hands rubbing my arm, back, shoulder, and the length of my leg. I feel how affected he is by the press of his hard cock against my hip.

"What about you?" I ask when I'm able to speak.

"Don't worry about me." He kisses the top of my head. "Not right now. I'm enjoying this."

At first, I don't understand his restraint. Then I remember. This is supposed to be a display of how I use toys. Completely professional. Maybe he doesn't want me.

I lift my heavy head and lean back against the cushions.

"Do you want to kiss me?" I ask, hoping maybe it isn't all professionalism at work here.

"Yes, but not yet."

The sting of rejection must show on my face, because he smiles when he says, "When I kiss you, I'm going to demand all your attention. No post-orgasmic high at the hands of quiet-and-unassuming over there. It's going to be all me."

The heat-seeking words strike my chest this time.

"Close your eyes and go to sleep. I'll be here when you wake up."

"I'm not tired," I say, my eyes closing as he traces lines over my eyebrows, my cheekbones, my jawline, my nose.

When I wake up nestled on Anders's lap and in his arms a while later, he's watching a vid with the volume low.

"Hungry?" he asks.

"Famished."

We finish the platter of cheese, crackers, and fruit. I slide my shorts on and close my cardigan as he retrieves the platter of snacks and refills our glasses. We while away the Sunday afternoon talking about how we were recruited for our jobs, the worst things we've ever eaten, and our various trips to Earth. He wants to visit nature preserves on his next visit back.

There's no mention of toys or replacement parts until we make plans to meet again later in the week.

7

Comparing Parts

Anders

A transgalactic message alert pings as I'm closing my shuttle schematics holovid.

"Accept message," I say as I close down my workstation for the day. The booming voice of my old friend and LovBot, Inc. liaison, Zephyr, fills my earpiece.

"'Lo, Anders. Greetings from Earth—I love saying that—I hope this message finds you drifting smoothly out there in the cosmos.

"You'll never believe what I found. A LovBot, model Colt 2.G.4 with parts compatible to your Frank-E bot. It's a newer design, but the couplings are often revamped from earlier models. Why reinvent the wheel every time, right? The Colt is revamped from the Frank-E model you were asking about."

A heavy weight drops in my stomach as Zeph continues his info-tribe, though Gwen will be happy to hear her bot can resume his duties.

"They're not cross-listed as compatible because the Colt-Ss didn't come on-line until after the Frank models were discontinued a while back. The Coltbot itself is useless. Its neuralnet processor is fried, but its parts are intact, and its loverod is still available. Apparently, it was a popular model. It's the first generation with silisynth-flesh coating, so its texture is more realistic than the Frank-E."

The message continues. "I can get it out to you on the next transport, so you could have it next month. Let me know if you'll still want it by then."

A whole month. The weight pressing against my chest eases. A lot can happen in that time. If I tell her the part is coming in, then I can ask her out without the complications of sex-based transaction casting a lecherous cloud on my intentions. What if she decides she doesn't need to explore relations beyond the mechanical kind, though? That would mean the end of our interactions. I'd like to avoid that possible outcome. If I hold off on telling her, we'll have more time getting to know each other, and I can surprise her if it's a success. While I wait to confirm that the part works, we can continue to explore all her options. Together. Win-win.

Or. I could tell Zephyr to keep it and not fix the bot at all.

I dismiss that thought as quickly as it pops into my head. That's not an option. Whatever happens with Gwen, lying is not the way to establish rapport with her.

I send Zephyr a quick note telling him to send the part. There's no guarantee it will work when it gets here. Gwen and I have a month before we know for sure. We're not due for another meeting until the weekend, but it would be good to strategize her goals before then.

I ping Gwen.

Gwen

The interns lean over my shoulder watching as I localize a cluster of nematodes on the screen. I no longer use the auto-function mode on Meemee to observe the microscopic creatures, allowing me to interact with nematode communities in unexpected ways. The interns have begun joining me to learn the new procedures we're developing.

Adapting the tech to use the features manually is turning out to be fun. The balance between tech and human innovation is gratifying. There's a reason the option to turn off auto features continues to be built into the tech, despite centuries of advancements in AI and biotech mimicry. Bio-organic life continues to surpass artificial design in innovative application.

My comm pings in my ear. It's Anders. I've been leaving it on while I work, waiting for updates on my bot. Or in case we need to meet in person, for any reason.

Stepping aside to let one of the interns manipulate the viewer, I leave them to continue their observations.

"I have news," he says when I open the comm.

I feel a slight thrill at the sound of his voice, but I brush it aside, focusing on his words. "News?"

"Yes. Can you meet to talk?"

My stomach skips at his words. "Of course."

"After work today? We can meet at the market on Fifth. That's on your way home, right?"

"Yes. It's where I usually pick up dinner." Before I can think about it too hard, I say, "We could eat in the market."

"Perfect!" His resonant voice booms into my earpiece. "Do you like Greek food?"

"Cerce's Celestial Café on the lower deck?"

"You know it?"

"Yes. It's a favorite of mine! I'm leaving work soon."

"Me too. I can be there around six thirty."

I end the comm without asking Anders about his news. He could've just told me over comms. I'm glad he didn't.

Anders

I arrive at the bistro first and find a table outside the restaurant on the promenade. The bustle of evening foot traffic milling through food carts and market vendors always makes for entertaining people watching.

This market is the most outwardly ethnically expressive gallery on the base. While many on the base wear uniforms or functional clothes, these shop owners and market vendors wear colorful garments from their home countries. There are other markets and food galleries, but this is the most colorful and artistically representative. Which is why it's always bustling. Gwen lives one level up and walks through the market on her way to and from work. It occurs to me that she may have chosen to live close to the market for this reason.

I move to dismiss the holoverts twirling over the table until I notice that one is announcing the café's plans for the Spring Fest.

Seasonal parties are celebrated with unparalleled zeal all over the base because they remind residents of Earth, nature, and the innate cycles that drive us. It's how we maintain our natural rhythms. They honor the patterns that are most rooted in our psyche as a species. Spring Fest is an explosion of life on this barge. The holobanners waving over the promenade also announce the festival in two weeks.

I leave the holovert on the table to twirl with wild abandon, possibly planting a seed for future meetings with Gwen.

I spot her wending her way through the crowd before she sees me. Her eyes are raised toward the second-story mezzanine, where shops and businesses line the gallery overlooking the promenade. When she drops her gaze, her eyes find me and her dimpled smile flashes like a solar flare.

"'Lo," she says as she approaches, and I stand to greet her.

"This is a great suggestion," she says as she sits. "I normally grab food on my way home. It's nice to sit outside."

After discussing our favorites on the menu, we agree to an assortment of dishes to share and enter them into the menu board embedded in the table.

"I got a message from a friend in Ohio."

"That's where LovBot is based, isn't it?" she asks, glancing around.

Ohio is a bot tech hub in the states, second only to Freetown Tech Designs in Sierra Leone.

"My contact found a part that's compatible with Frank-E."

Her brow furrows, and she doesn't respond right away. I expected her to be more excited. Or relieved. Enthusiastic? Her expression is more perplexed than happy.

"I thought you'd want to know," I say, breaking the silence.

The promenade is bustling and loud. I'm not worried about being overheard, but for Gwen's discretion, I don't go into more explicit detail.

"Of course. This is great news. Does it do everything I want?"

A servebot delivers plates with an assortment of hummus, dolmas, spanako-pita bites, roasted red peppers, and other shareables. Gwen pours our wine while I partition out samples onto our plates.

"It's a newer model. It doesn't do everything, but the skin is more realistic. Like the one I loaned you."

A faint blush colors her cheeks, and I smile, remembering the way she'd demonstrated how she used the toy for me.

"Are you sure it will work?" she asks.

"No, I'm not, actually." I'm surprised and relieved her questions take this direction. "The part's compatible, but we can't be certain that connectivity between Frank-E's control center and the part wasn't damaged."

"Then shouldn't we keep looking at other options?" she asks.

"Yes," I say, leaning forward, energized by a wave of relief at her suggestion.

"Just in case," she adds.

"Absolutely." A relieved laugh escapes me.

"What can you tell me about it?"

"It has a newer coating. It feels like the real thing."

"I don't really have a basis for comparison ..." she says with a muffled snort. "Since it's been so long ..." She trails off, looking away.

The casual trust with which she tosses out the comment warms my chest. A hundred not-so-subtle jokes about her needing to feel the real thing come to mind, but I bite them back, not wanting to discourage her.

"All you have to do is ask for what you want." My suggestion is vague. I don't know what she'd ask for, but whatever she wants, I'll find a way to make it happen.

She flashes a sad smile at that, but it disappears so quickly I'm not sure it was sad at all.

She lifts her chin, and her gaze travels to the mezzanine, where the lights begin to glint as the room dims to simulate an evening on Earth. One of many patterns designed to make us feel at home.

The low light is reminiscent of the peachy hue of a setting sun, and when her gaze returns to me, her skin glows in the soft light.

"It's more a curiosity," she leans in and says in a quiet voice, "but I'd like to be able to compare."

The words that roll off her plump pink lips send my imagination spiraling.

Gwen

His mouth opens. Then it closes. Then opens again. After a long while it closes again.

I broke him. My heart pounds erratically, and I go into a little panic. He understands my meaning, but maybe I've gone too far.

"Just to be clear, are you saying you want to compare your bot part, Frank-E's manpart, with the real thing? My real thing?"

Put like that, I've crossed a line. Even though I myself demonstrated my own parts recently. He's seen me. He's held me. Exposed and at my most vulnerable. I'm not asking for anything different. *In the interest of research*, I want to say, but that wouldn't be the truth.

And he had been affected in the moment too. I saw that myself.

My shrug is casual, though I am far from it. My heart is racing. The last time I asked for what I wanted, my life changed. But I'm not asking for life altering.

He swallows and smiles. "Are you asking me to show you mine? ... Well, since you did show me yours ..." he says, his fluster gone and the twinkle back in his eye.

"I am," I say, feeling the need to assert myself. "I'm sure you'd enjoy it."

That I have to convince him to show me his quells my hard-fought boldness. But I don't back down. I do want to compare. To see him. Touch him. Taste him.

He must see something in my expression, because his wicked grin eases into a soft smile. My normally light-hearted, joking doctor turns serious. "Where? When? How, exactly?"

"I don't want to pressure you." My heart pounds, and I feel heat rise in my face.

He laughs and his voice is a low rumble when he asks, "Should we get this to go?"

In my quarters, Anders sets the carry-out caddy with our unfinished dinner on the table in the mealprep and then joins me in the living.

"How would you like to proceed?" he asks, putting me in control.

I take his hand and lead him to the sofa. I leave him there while I go get the vibrator. When I return, he hasn't moved. I set it on the coffee table.

"Do you want me to undress, or would you like to do it?"

I want to watch him, so I say, "Would you?"

He stands in front of the couch and unfastens his collarless tunic. As he sets it aside, I admire his toned chest. He's nothing like the over-muscled machines we looked at on his holovid. His chest is dusted with strawberry-blond hair. My gaze flicks to his before dropping back down to watch him unfasten his pants.

He slides them down his hips and his already hard cock pops out and bobs. His pants drop and he steps out of them, setting them aside with his tunic.

He positions himself on the center cushion, his legs spread and his arms draped over the back of the sofa with an arrogant grace. The gesture is regal and entitled, but he's exposing himself, putting himself on display and at my mercy. It's not swagger but a show of vulnerability and trust. My heart pounds against my chest, and I feel my pulse in my whole body.

His erect cock stands at attention, and I can't take my eyes off him.

I kneel on the floor between his legs. He's long and thick, his head an angry purple and the vein under his upright shaft pulsing. I lift my gaze from his beautiful dick to his eyes. He wears a proud smirk. His cock bobs at me and I laugh, breaking the sultry tension filling the room.

"I'm all yours," he says.

It has been so long. I take my time. I reach out and trace my finger along the bulging vein, and he hisses at my touch. I raise my eyes to watch his expression as I cup his balls and gently roll them in their protective sack with gentle fingers. I was wrong. This soft texture can't be replicated with silicon composites.

He breathes out on a hum while I return my full attention to study the gorgeous specimen before me. I grip him, slowly sliding my fingertips along the soft yet hard shaft until I'm tracing his wide head. His body tightens. I don't mean to tease, but I want to take my time.

There's precum at the tip, and I can't help smiling as I flash a quick look to his face. With his eyes locked on my fingers, I spread the bead of cum around his head.

I wrap my fingers around him and slide the fleshy skin up and down in slow, deliberate movements.

"Stroke me," he moans, and I glance at his face again. His lids are heavy while he watches my hand.

He wraps his hand over mine and, squeezing, guides my hand to the tip, showing me what he likes.

His moan sounds like he's in pain, but his face is flushed.

"Can I taste?" I ask.

"Yes," he croaks out.

I kiss the tip before licking the bead of cum. I spread my lips and wrap them around his head. I experiment, biting gently.

He smiles through a moan. "Be careful there."

I kiss him again before licking my lips and taking him into my mouth, this time deeper. I swirl my tongue, spreading my spit around.

"You taste good," I say, pulling away for a moment. "Much better than your toy." Then I slip him back inside, swirling my tongue.

"You put it in your mouth?" he asks on another croak.

I nod as much as I can with his cock in my mouth, not releasing him.

"Such a dirty girl," he says.

His words work their magic and every nerve ending in my body lights up.

I take as much of him as I can and fuck him with my mouth, drooling and moaning and sucking on him as I grip the base of his shaft. Taking breaths when I can, I work his cock gracelessly to drive him toward release, until finally he moans, and I feel his balls tighten in my hand.

He's gripping the couch cushions, and I look into his face, which is twisted into an ecstatic grimace. I release his balls and take one of his hands in mine, raising it to cup the back of my head. I clasp his fingers with mine, showing him how I want him to grip my hair. Then I drop my head down on his cock, taking him as deep as I can.

Understanding crosses his face, and he holds my head in place as he begins bucking his hips upward, fucking my mouth.

I moan around his length as he takes control. He bucks a few times, fucking my mouth in shallow thrusts before he begins to deepen his motion, until he's finally hitting the back of my throat. I work to take him, reveling in the sensation of being used.

"I'm going to cum," he says at length.

I hum my encouragement around his cock. I move my hands to either side of him on the cushion, giving him complete access to move my head as he likes.

He releases in a loud succession of grunts and pleased curses as he cums down my throat. I choke a little around him and he releases me, pulling out of my mouth.

Anders's body relaxes in a puddle, overcome with lethargy, and I can't resist giving his messy, flagging cock a little kiss.

"I'm not sure that the part is going to feel that soft," I say, pleased by the dopey expression on his face.

"No," he says, and mutters something that sounds like, "I can't imagine it will."

He pulls me into his lap. We don't say anything for a long time. He looks at my mouth and licks his lips. But he makes no move to kiss me.

"Would you like me to—"

"I'll see you Saturday to look at bots?" I interrupt him. I don't need reciprocation. I just want him to enjoy. I liked making him feel good. I liked watching his face contort with barefaced rapture. I want to tell him that when he leaves, I'll pleasure myself with his toy. But I don't.

"Yes," he says in a low, sleepy voice. His fingers stroke my hair, and we lie there for a long time. I can tell he's dozing beneath me when I sense his breath settle into a deep, steady cadence. But he wakes with a start after a few minutes, apologizing for falling asleep.

"Do you want to take some of the food home?"

"We can finish it together, if you're hungry," he suggests.

He retreats to the hygiene to clean himself up while I lay out the remains of our dinner.

We eat in companionable silence for a while. "I want to know what else you like," he says, interrupting the quiet.

"I liked *that*," I say simply, meaning it.

When he leaves, we agree to look at bot models on Saturday.

8

The Truth About Humans and LovBots

Gwen

When I arrive at Anders's workshop, he greets me with the enthusiasm of a puppy.

"I'm not ready, but I made dinner," he says, wiping his hands on a dish towel. "Would you like to join me?"

"I'd hate to intrude. I can come back."

"I made enough to share. Please keep me company so I don't have to eat alone."

"I enjoy eating alone," I say. I'm used to it.

"That doesn't surprise me." His eyes crinkle at the corners. His impish grin doesn't make me feel defensive. "I don't mind eating alone either, but I like your company."

I can't help the smile that spreads across my face. His eyes drop to my mouth. He winds the dishcloth tight around his fist, but the humor in his eyes never falters. I smile more during our meetings than any other part of the day.

"I was going to heat premade soup from the market at home for dinner, but this smells so much better." The scent of garlic, yeasty bread, and savory home cooking wafts from behind him, and I realize he planned this. It—he—is too delicious to walk away from. "Okay."

He gestures toward the back door of his workshop to his residence.

Entering Anders's quarters, I'm surprised to see his softer, cheerier side on display. Overstuffed seats, plush carpets in neutral tones, and colorful throw cushions soften the otherwise austere quarters. The sofa is blue-green and the walls are light blue, friendlier than the slate grays or beiges that base residents often choose. The art screens show spectacular images of nebulas from the black, probably taken by cameras on the base. He reveals a part of himself that other clients may not get to see, and I feel excitement at having access to this private piece of him.

I'm wearing a flowy skirt, shorter than my usual. My silky, thin top clings to me, caressing my skin, and my bambasynth cardigan, made from a genetically modified bamboo fiber, is light with an appealing drape. I'm often cold in the common spaces on the base, and I normally dress for those temps. Anders's workshop is always warm—or maybe it's him. My choice has nothing to do with the way the silky fabrics flatters my curves, it's all about practicality and comfort.

He leads me to the dining, which marks a boundary between the open floor plan mealprep and the living, set with place settings for two. When he extracts a casser'dish from the multicooker, he presents it with a dramatic flourish.

"I hope you like lasagna. Vegetarian."

"Yes, that's great. That was thoughtful of you."

The warmth of the lasagna, cooked with me in mind, permeates my chest and satisfies a hunger I didn't know lived there. I can't hide my grin.

He sets out a simple salad that compliments the complexity of the lasagna. "Would you like wine?"

I accept with a nod, and he brings over two wine glasses and two bottles of wine, a white and a red, along with two large glasses of water.

I savor every word of our conversation with each bite of the rich, textured pasta dish. He peppers me with questions about my work and what brought me to the base. I tell him I'd been recruited after graduate school, and how I couldn't resist the lure of cutting-edge agricultural biotech.

He's a second-generation resident of the starbase. He went to college and graduate school on Earth, and his parents retired there, but he jumped at the chance to return when Katana recruited him. The base was home to him, and he would've come back, even if Katana Corp hadn't offered him his dream job.

"Do you ever visit Earth?" I ask.

"I do. Don't get me wrong. It's beautiful. But when I'm there, I have the sense that I'm bound. Here I feel free. Maybe it's the gravity on Earth. Or maybe it's just that this is home to me."

"That's curious," I say, taking the last bite of my second piece of lasagna. "I feel the opposite. On Earth it feels expansive and limitless. Here, I'm cocooned in. Not that I mind it. The gardens in the agradomes keep me from feeling cooped up."

We talk about his work on the vessels tested on the base. What he can tell me, at least—most of his work is classified. I tell him about my shy nematodes and how introducing them on the base has increased agricultural growth, which serves both the agradomes on the base and food production on Earth.

"I'm stuffed," I say. "I don't know how much"—I almost say 'work,' but it's hardly work—"I'll be able to do after that meal."

We planned to look at bot models. All day long I imagined more hands-on demonstrations and comparisons of bot parts. Instead, the lasagna is heavy, and I'm sated and sedate.

"We don't have to rush." He leans back in his chair and stretches his long legs. "Maybe in a little while. We can just talk a bit. I made dessert too. Tiramisu."

My eyes bulge, and he laughs. "It never occurs to me to cook with all the food options available to us, not that I can cook. But you bake too?" I ask.

"I love to cook. Feeding people makes me happy," he says with a wink, feeding that mysterious hunger in my chest, higher than where'd I'd expect to feel lust in my belly.

"That's not a secret you keep well."

Anders

We don't linger long at the table before we move to the sitting area.

"I thought you'd like to look at my own bot, a newer model. See what the options are." *Maybe start letting go of Frank-E.* I keep that thought to myself.

"You have a bot?"

"I do. He's not the latest, but he's newer than your model." I call out to the room, "Simon, come in here please?"

The door to the room adjacent to my workshop slides open, and Simon emerges.

"A manbot?"

I lean back on the sofa and spread my arms across the back, enjoying the curious expression playing across her face. I could watch her for hours.

Gwen is submissive. She responds beautifully to my commands. Something deep down inside her wants me to take control. The way she wanted me to grip her hair and use her mouth revealed so much about her needs. And that she's aware of those needs.

I normally meet my partners in the club. It's the most convenient and all our expectations are out in the open. I've rarely felt the pull to pursue a relationship, but when I have, we've started off with some awareness of each other's kinks. My work doesn't allow much time for socializing outside the club.

Now is the time to tell her about the club. If we're getting to know each other, certain details have to come out now. I don't know how she feels about kink beyond the capabilities of a sexbot.

But if the way she's responded to me so far is any indication, this could be a good thing.

I watch her face closely to gauge her reaction when I say, "I'm a Dominant."

I hold my breath, waiting for a reaction.

She doesn't give me one for a long time before she finally leans forward and asks, "Really?"

9

Human versus LovBot

Gwen

I 'm submissive. I know this from my research. I was in a BDSM relationship. But the revelation of what I wanted ended what I thought was a contented relationship. We weren't in love, but I didn't know that until it was all over. When all was said and done, my heart was untouched. I'd invested six years of my life in a relationship that had been a convenient arrangement. One that had made sense in grad school but left barely a dent emotionally when it was done. I didn't get anything out of that relationship I can't get with my bot. He satisfies all the needs my ex did. He's sufficient.

My mind trips over all the implications of Anders's revelation. Excitement. Fear. Curiosity. Doubt.

When I don't respond, he continues. "Sometimes I bring partners here." His eyes are fixed on me, studying me. "I like to incorporate a sexbot in our play."

The way we did the other day, he doesn't say, but a ghost of the words flutters over my skin as my body understands exactly how he uses bots in his sex play.

Partners. With an S. How many submissives does he have? It's not the most important question, but it's the one that burns in my chest. I force myself to suppress the rising wave of jealousy. "Do you entertain a lot of women? People?" My voice is soft, but curious. Where is this jealousy coming from?

"No. None at all." He's quick to answer. "I haven't ... uh ... played in a while ..."

The choked feeling in my chest eases a little. The jealousy flitters over me, and I force it down. I have no claim on Anders beyond professional.

"I've had arrangements that were exclusive, as well as casual arrangements, but there is no one in my life right now."

He leans forward and holds his hands open to me. This is where Anders confounds me. His commanding presence could take, but instead he invites. He presents me the choice. He invites my questions. My old curiosity creeps back in, and I rest my hands in his.

Anders traces his thumbs over the backs of my hands and says, "Gwen, would you like to look at Simon?"

My name on his lips is hypnotic, and it takes me a minute to process his question. "Yes. Of course. It's why I'm here."

"I thought you'd like to compare the oral features of your bot with a different bot."

"How?"

"Simon."

"What do you have in mind?"

"Right here. It'll take me a minute to set up."

"Okay." Heat blasts through me with a full-body blush.

My thoughts vacillate between old fantasies of exploring BDSM and the reality of my experience with my ex.

A moment later, Anders has a long, padded table covered in a black sheet set up in the middle of the living. Pushing thoughts of the past aside, I stand next to the table.

"Roxy, low lights," he says to the room, and the soft light grows dim.

"Take off your shirt and lie on the table."

I wait for him to turn around, but he doesn't. He watches. I half expect him to help me, but once again he doesn't touch me. Gooseflesh erupts on my skin with little more than his gaze on my body.

"You mentioned that your bot's tongue secretes oil. You're okay if we use massage oil?"

"Yes," I say as I drape my cardigan and top over the back of an armchair.

I unclasp my bra, and once I've set it with my top, I stand naked from the waist up. The weight of his gaze is a caress. I lie on the table.

Standing over me, he says, "Hold onto the sides of the table. Don't let go."

I tremble with eagerness.

"Yes," I say, gripping the sides of the table.

"Good girl."

My nipples tighten at his praise, and I flush with warmth.

"Simon, attend to Gwen's breast please." The request is functional and entirely unsexy. Maybe he's trying to maintain professional separation.

I glance over to find him watching me with a mischievous smirk. He's toying with me.

Simon appears over me. He lowers his face to my chest, his mouth opening unnaturally wide to cover one breast. The sight incites more fear than lust. The tongue secretes an oil. The bot strokes my nipple with its tongue as gentle suction pulls at my breast. The tongue flicks my nipple then swirls around it, followed by more suction. It repeats the flick, swirl, suck sequence and soon falls into a steady pattern.

It's a pleasant sensation, but I rarely use this feature on my bot. Any heat I feel as I lie on the table comes from Anders's speculative gaze.

"How would you like to compare that to a human mouth?"

His words send a zing of lust shooting to my core.

"Yes, please."

"Tell me what you want."

"What?" I ask, confused. I just did, didn't I?

He leans in close, his breath fanning over my ear and in my hair.

"Tell me to lick your nipple."

My words trip over each other, coming out in a breathless rush. "Lick my nipple."

With a crinkly-eyed smirk, he strokes the underside of the breast that isn't being attended to by the bot. He lowers his mouth to my breast and kisses my nipple with a gentleness that belies the heat in his eyes. Then his lips wrap around the puckered areola and nipple, and I feel a gentle tug as he sucks. He swipes his tongue over the peak before nipping with his teeth. He does not fall into a steady rhythm. His flicks and sucks are wet, messy, and erratic.

Everything else falls away as he makes love to my breast. And it loves him back, responds to him. My back arches involuntarily, my body wanting to give more of itself to him.

He moans against my skin with such appreciation that my knees rise and fall open in a natural response.

He squeezes the underside of my breast with his hand and releases my tight bud with a pop. "Is that an invitation?" he asks, eyeing my legs.

I start to close them but stop myself. "I guess it is," I say. I'm panting now.

"Well, Tiger, would you like to try oral stimulation on your cunt?"

I shiver under his gaze as his words stoke a need he's been kindling since I arrived. Like a line linked to the nerves in my core.

His tongue sweeps out and swipes my nipple again as his finger strokes my breast.

"Yes," I say.

"Would you prefer LovBot or human mouth?"

I don't have to think about it. "Yours."

"Tell me what you want."

I'm confused by his need to have me repeat everything. Regardless, my pelvis rocks toward him, and my pussy pulses, liking the game. I can't tell if I'm irritated or needy. "I just told you."

"Say the words, Little Tiger. 'Lick my cunt.'"

His low voice strums the taut cord wound through me. "Lick my cunt ..." I almost say *sir*. "... Anders."

He groans softly and says, "Simon, desist."

The bot stops its rhythmic ministrations, stands erect, and steps back. Anders pulls the sheet beneath me, dragging me to the end of the table and settling my ass at the edge. With smooth efficiency, Anders slides my panties off, gathers my skirt at my waist, and pushes my knees toward my shoulders.

"Hold your knees. Don't let go."

Exposed to him, the air chills my already wet pussy and I tremble. I grasp my legs behind the knees and spread them wide for him.

"Good girl," he groans.

He steps away and grabs a stool. He repositions himself at the foot of the table and settles in. I feel warm fingers spread my folds, and then his tongue drags leisurely from my ass to my clit, coating me with my own moisture.

A breathy "Stars" escapes my lips. At that, he attacks my cunt like he's starving. His tongue dips inside, licking and tasting. Then he moves his focus to my clit, which he laps at with the flat of his tongue several times before circling the nub.

It's delicious chaos, and I can't help rocking my hips. Then I feel his fingers at the entrance of my channel. He applies pressure at the edge, teasing me, but doesn't enter.

"Tell me, Tiger, what do you need?" His breath is hot against my pussy.

"Please, Anders, go inside."

"Tell me to finger you."

"Oh gods," I pant. "I need. Please, finger me."

One finger plunges inside, then two. He slides in and out with a measured pace as he licks and nuzzles my nub. I buck against his mouth as he drives his fingers inside me, drawing the cord in me tighter and tighter.

"Anders," I moan.

He curls his fingers and strokes my inner walls as his other hand runs over the back of my thighs, squeezes my ass, and works its way to my breast. Massage oil coats my breast where Simon worked on me. Anders cups my breast firmly and rubs the oil into my skin. He squeezes my nipple and my inner walls pulse around the fingers of his other hand. He quickens his pace, fucking me harder with his hand.

"It doesn't take long, does it, Tiger? You just need the right touch."

I agree with an animalistic grunt as I pulse around his fingers.

He brings his free hand down to my ass and gives it a light smack. The slight sting sends a jolt to my pussy then dissipates, leaving a pulsing heat in its place.

"I'm here, beautiful. Let go. I'll catch you."

He pumps his fingers harder and flicks my clit faster with his tongue. It's not long before the taut cord holding me together snaps and I come undone. He continues to pump and lick as pleasure reverberates through my body and radiates out of me in sensuous waves.

I release my legs, and he drapes them over his shoulders. He strokes my inner thigh as he coaxes the final ripples of my orgasm through me.

With a smug expression, he peers up at me from between my legs. "So, which do you prefer? Human or bot?"

"I'll need to conduct more research," I whisper.

Anders

I slide her off the table and set her on her feet. Her skirt falls into place, her breasts still exposed to me. She's stunning. Her bun is coming undone, so I reach behind her and find the clasp binding it. When I pop it open and slide it out, I'm rewarded with a cascade of dark wavy curls spilling over her shoulders.

"You are beautiful, you know that?"

She turns her face to me. I'm lost in her bright, dimpled smile and sparkling eyes.

The need to claim her mouth and tell her she's mine grips me, but I resist and look away before my eyes give away too much. I want our first kiss to be one we tell our grandchildren about.

10

Feelings for Humans

Anders

I should go," she says. The dazed expression on her face clears, and though she still looks sleepy, that sharp clarity returns to her eyes.

"What?" I step back but don't let go. I study her face, looking for anything to explain her change in mood. "Why?"

We stand in my sitting area. She's topless and disheveled in my arms, having experienced what looked like a spectacular orgasm, and she wants to leave? Sub drop? Is she suffering from post-orgasmic depression? If she is, it's sudden.

"Well, we've discovered a few things about what I like, right?" She steps out from the enclosure of my arms, and I release her reluctantly. She slips her silky blouse on. Her breasts jiggle as she pulls her top over her head, and they disappear from sight. She doesn't bother with her bra, and her nipples poke through the thin fabric. I resist the urge to pull her into my arms again.

"Yes," I say, baffled by her sudden retreat. "So?"

"So, don't you have everything you need? Wasn't that the whole point?"

My heart becomes lead.

"No. That wasn't the whole point. I hope you got some enjoyment out of it." *I don't have everything I need. I need you*, I don't say. I can't let her orgasm and leave. "How about dessert?" I ask, floundering for the first time maybe ever.

She smiles, but it's weak. No dimples. "I'm still full."

Something is wrong. I offended her. I'm losing her.

"Come sit," I say. "Let's look at bots while you're here. It's still early." I call out to the room, "Roxy. Vid screen. Sofa, please."

I lead Gwen to the sofa where a holographic screen appears. She steps through the screen and takes the end seat against the armrest. She looks small, no longer the radiant star that lost herself cumming for me.

Maybe it is mild sub drop. I sit next to her. "I want to make sure you're okay. Let me take care of you for a little while before you go."

She lets out a breathy laugh, and I put my hand out to her. Her smile is still small, lacking any hint of dimple, as she slips her hand into mine.

Gwen

This is how Dominants—with a capital D—take care of their subs. This is what I'd read about. The importance of aftercare. The way his Dominant brain kicks in to take care of me is sweet and reassuring. But it doesn't assuage the feeling of having the bottom drop out from beneath me.

"Please don't worry," I say. "This isn't sub drop."

I know what sub drop is from my research. My sadness doesn't come from a post-orgasmic crash. Or maybe it does. When he looked at me with eyes that wanted to eat me, I was sure he would kiss me. I wasn't prepared for how much I wanted it. Then he looked away. Of course. I'm a client, and he doesn't want to cross that line. I understand that. For a moment, I forgot that I don't want to cross that line either.

I'm not a masochist. Not in the physical sense nor the emotional.

I refocus on our goals. Maybe lack of human touch has left me vulnerable and desperate. I need to get a grip. This contact with Anders has been good for me.

I needed this, but I don't need to get attached. *Focus on your objective*, I remind myself. Just like Anders does. With his team of submissives.

"Roxy, show us 'LovBots, samples, selection one,' please." Anders's voice is calm and reassuring.

Pictures of abnormally large human-style droids appear on the screen, and my laugh bursts out of me in an unexpected gust. Just like that, my tension leaves my body.

"You selected these?"

"Yes. I knew you'd like them. They are completely unassuming."

The distraction is welcome, and it's clear that we're of the same view. It's like he senses my need to recalibrate myself.

"Does that one have a sixteen-pack?" I ask. "Is that anatomically possible?"

The worry leaves his face. "I think they gave his muscles muscles," he says, inspecting the model on the holoview.

"You reviewed their penis attachment specifications? Do their penises have penises?"

It's his turn to laugh, the tension leaving his shoulders. His crinkly smile returns. "In the interest of research." He rests his arm across the back of the couch, enclosing me but not crowding.

"Of course. What have you found?"

"I also looked at their mouth specs."

"Oh" escapes me on a gasp. The reminder of tonight's demonstration crashes against the seawall I've started rebuilding. Despite my attempts to focus my mind on the bot samples, the memory of Anders's mouth on me lingers on my body.

He glances down and gives me a reassuring wink. "I also have a selection of furries and alien species for your consideration."

I burst out another surprised laugh. No matter what happens, I can enjoy this man's company. We can be friends. Thoughts of his warm skin, strong hands, and crinkly smile will carry me for a long time to come, replacing the memories I came here with.

I pull myself out of my memories, rampant need creating chaos in my stomach. And lower. His lips. His tongue. His hands. Everything I want. Need. Fantasize about.

I need to recalibrate.

Extracting myself from the chaos of escalating heat, I struggle to reinforce my walls.

"Why don't we resume looking at bots next time?" I say.

His lips purse, but he nods, confusion playing over his face.

Anders

The shadow clouding the sparkle in her eyes clears away, and she gifts me a sweet expression of ready curiosity.

Fuck it. If I keep passing on kissable moments for the purpose of creating memories, I'm going to miss all the moments with her.

I drop my head and touch my lips to hers. She parts her mouth for me. I kiss her bottom lip and suck softly. She kisses and sucks at my top lip in return.

I open my mouth to her and let her explore. She dips her tongue in, finding mine, then retreats, taunting me to follow. I do, losing myself to the kiss. I lick and suck, reveling in the feel of her mouth on mine. Her soft lips are playful and sure, despite her reserved nature. She may be submissive, but my scientist loves to play. A breath of life in the solitude of the black.

Consumed by her soft floral scent, lavender and earthy herbs, I'm hers.

11

Coupling Mishaps

Anders

In my workshop a week later, I open Zeph's package with some hesitation. Part of me wants to sit on the package for a few days, but the sooner I get the job done, the sooner we'll be able to move forward without the specter of an adequately satisfying sexbot hanging over my head.

I extract Frank-E's replacement penis from the box. When I see it, my first impulse is to put it back in the box and put it into storage.

I ping her to invite her to let her know.

"'Lo," she says when she answers the vid on the second ping.

"Guess what came in today."

The look she gives me is blank. She says nothing for a prolonged minute before saying with a weak smile, "So soon?"

"My contact at LovBot managed to catch the shuttle delivery before it left the same day he called. It's here two weeks earlier than expected."

"That's great." Her tone is as flat as my mood, and I entertain a fanciful notion that maybe she doesn't want the project to end either. But I shove that idea aside. It doesn't matter. *Get it done, then see about dinner when you're no longer her service tech.*

"Do you want to help me prep it before we install it? At my workshop on Saturday?"

I have the coupler component, so swapping them out will take a matter of minutes. Installing the new Dat.Ch, the data chip containing Frank-E's stored data, is a little more involved, but also a piece of cake.

"Yeah," she says, her smile returning. "That would be great."

Saturday morning, she arrives prompt as usual with a box of pastries from the French bakery at the market.

"So what can I do to help?" Ever curious, she's champing at the bit to see the inner workings.

"To start, keep me company. You probably want to inspect the part?"

"Sure," she says, craning her graceful neck to view the components spread over the table.

I run a cable from an electronics console on my workbench and plug it into the base of the penis.

She holds the part in her delicate hands as I work the control center, which functions like Frank-E's brain to send signals to his extremities.

"It has different sizes like Frank-E's old one."

The part grows to its largest size, and my cock springs to life as she wraps her fingers around its increasing girth.

"Its largest setting is larger than Frank-E's," I say, my gaze landing on her delicate, probing fingers as she pinches the mushroom-shaped tip.

I force myself to look away, and I adjust the controls.

She gasps. "Oh, that's cold."

"It gets to freezing, like ice cubes," I explain. "They've sent another coupling. Mostly we need to swap out the connector on this part and replace it with Frank-E's old one. I've cleaned it. Then it will be a matter of making sure Frank-E's computer can link to the part."

Gwen

Anders detaches the cable and disconnects the internal mechanism of the new part from its silisynth sheath.

Watching him adeptly make minor adjustments to the connectors has me imagining all the things he can do with those long, talented fingers.

He looks up at me, and I blush like I've been caught. He smiles. "Now, where has that curious mind wandered to?"

"I'm just wondering if it'll link to Frank-E's systems."

"Getting excited?"

I blush again. My thoughts weren't about Frank-E.

I watch him disconnect an end cap and extract the core out of the interior shell as I worry the soft silisynth sleeve between my fingers. It is softer than Frank-E's skin coating.

I have mixed feelings. I'm excited for this new part, which disassembled seems far more complex than the toys I keep in my drawer. He disconnects a few chips and begins to solder in a replacement electronic component.

"What's that?" I ask.

"It's the Dat.Ch that should communicate with Frank-Es' central processor. If the parts are compatible, they will talk to each other."

"Does it have the extending thrust feature?"

"Sadly, it doesn't. But it has a changeable texture. You can have a smooth surface, ribbed surface, or rippling surface."

I bite my lip. The textures don't replace the soft warmth of Anders's flesh.

I imagine the possibilities while Anders watches me. My face heats. Anders smiles. Looking away, I pick up a titanium ring that fits in the palm of my hand and trace a line around the cool metal.

"What's this?"

"It's the coupler ring. It's what holds the part in place." He holds up Frank-E's new penis. "It's ready. Should we go see if it will integrate with Frank-E's central processor?"

"What? Now?" I hadn't expected to fix Frank-E so soon. But Anders is eager to test the part. To complete the project. Maybe he's happy to put this ongoing job behind him. The twinge of sadness that's haunted me since the part came in flares up.

"There's no better time."

"Of course." Anders wraps the phallus in a stericloth and tucks it into a tool case with some attachment components and the tools he'll need.

"Let's go."

I hand him the coupler, and he slips it into the magzip pocket on the outside of the bag.

As we walk through the market, Anders says, "Maybe we should pick up some lunch in the market? To celebrate?"

We're coming to the end. Once Frank-E is fixed, there won't be any more reason to meet. At least not for Anders. Distracted, I agree to pick up lunch. I can't shake the coldness that overtakes me.

Hundreds of niggling curiosities arise in my mind. Questions I thought I'd have time to ask but kept to myself. The club being one of the main questions.

"When you say bring subs to your place, what do you mean?" That little jealousy trickles up, but I push it aside, focusing on the club. *There's a place where I could go to experiment?* The thought sends a frisson through my body. I try to imagine faceless strangers, but the strangers all morph into Anders.

"I'm a member of a private club that caters to members' intimate desires. Normally, I play at the club, but sometimes if I'm working on a particular design or want to test out products, I bring the occasional member home."

I glance around the market, trying to act casual. "How do you meet subs? At the club, I mean?"

Anders answers, "Everything's pretty straightforward at the club. We're all there for more or less the same thing. It takes the guesswork out of meeting people."

He studies my face. I look away, feeling heat rise in my cheeks. "Are you interested in checking it out?"

"I was just curious," I say. His gaze on me is like the magnifier lens mounted on his workbench. "But yes."

His lips tighten into a line. He doesn't want me to go. Or maybe he doesn't want to go with me. But I could get the contact information from him.

Anders

Our entire interaction has been sex-based by the nature of this project. The club would just be an extension of that. I want more. I want us to get to know each other. Just us. Outside of a sexual context, at first. I want to take her to the club, but not yet.

Back at Gwen's, we set our dinner aside for later, and I set to work on Frank-E.

After opening the stericloth out on the coffee table and putting out the parts I'll need, I crouch over Frank-E's pelvic area to investigate the cavity where I'll insert his upgrade.

Gwen

Anders leans over Frank-E, his headlamp spotlighting the electronics within the bot's pelvis unit.

This is it. Once he fixes Frank-E, he'll be done.

With a small hand compressor, he blows air into the cavity to blow out any particulates.

Peering over his shoulder, I'm close enough to smell his scent. Something natural that reminds me of Earth. He mentioned he runs in the gardens, and I'm overwhelmed by the desire to run with him on the trails that circle the grove in the central gardens. What would that be like? A morning run followed by a coffee in the market.

The pockets of the tool case behind Anders are all open, and I spy the coupler. On impulse, I snatch the coupler and slip it into the oversized pocket of my cardigan.

He tinkers in Frank-E's pelvic cavity, inserting his electrical grippers and then inserting the Dat.Ch. He turns and looks at the table. When he doesn't find what he's looking for, he pulls his tool bag closer and inspects the pockets.

His brow furrows. "That's weird. I could've sworn I'd grabbed the coupler."

"That *is* weird," I say. I lie without lying. And a sick feeling settles in my gut. I can't give it to him now. He'll see me take it out of my pocket.

"Maybe I dropped it," he says, looking under the sofa.

"Maybe," I say. "But we would've heard it fall, I think."

"Yeah. Maybe I left it on my workbench. I can run back and grab it and be back soon."

"Oh, don't go to all the trouble. You can finish it later."

He opens his mouth as if to insist, and then seems to rethink it. "Okay. As long as you're not in a hurry."

Looking into his big earnest eyes, what little I've eaten becomes heavy in my gut and starts eating at me. I should pretend to find it, but I don't want him to finish and leave.

I could tell him the truth, but then he'd think I'm a nut. After all the trouble we'd gone through and then stealing the part. I couldn't even explain it to myself. I'm never impulsive like this.

"To be honest, I'm a little nervous," I say, offering the little admission, not that it mitigates my lie.

Eyebrows furrowed, he directs Frank-E to remove himself from the couch and sits down in the vacated spot.

I clarify. "About the changes. I've been used to things. Frank-E's part. Doing things a certain way for so long. And it's about to change."

A sympathetic expression crosses his face. "That makes sense."

He peers up at me from the couch with a curious look.

"Would you like something to drink? I have wine. And beer." Which I'd bought on the off chance he'd come back.

"A beer would be great," he says, packing his tools into his case as I turn to retrieve our drinks.

Tension lifted, I return with our drinks and the carry-tote with our lunch.

"Could you tell me more about the club you're a member of?"

He stretches his arm along the back of the sofa and tilts his bottle back. His throat bobs as he takes a long swig. When he lowers the bottle, he meets my gaze again. "You are curious, aren't you?"

12

LovBots Don't Lie

Anders

When I return home, the coupler ring isn't on the workbench. I retrace the moments before I left my workshop with Gwen.

I imagine myself setting out the cloth and wrapping Frank-E's part and the attachment components. I remember tucking the ring, which fits in the palm of my hand, into the magzip pocket outside my case. She was standing here next to me while we worked on Frank-E's part. I packed my tools. She handed me the coupler. She was distracting, fingering each of the components on the table the way she was, delicate fingers edging the ring. It's possible I set it aside without noticing. But it's not on any visible surfaces.

I unpack my case, putting away my tools and confirming that the coupler isn't in any of those drawers. I dispose of wire shavings and scrap. I peek into the recycler, which only has the remains of today's work. No coupler.

It had been an afterthought. I didn't want to fold it in the stericloth because I didn't want it to get bent, and the pocket was empty so there was no danger of harm. I'm sure of it.

The zipper was closed when I arrived at Gwen's. I remember unzipping it and seeing it in the pocket.

Maybe she took it. But why? She was so insistent on fixing Frank-E. But I can't shake the idea. Why would she do that?

It must be in her quarters. A grin spreads across my face. I'll just have to go back and look.

Gwen

Maybe my nematodes have burrowed into my brain and reduced me to a zombified, unthinking state? Unlikely. I still can't believe I took it.

I could tell him I found it on the floor. We looked everywhere, but I could say it rolled away. My stomach roils at my deception.

I could sneak the coupler back into his bag. I can't tell him I found it here. It would be too obvious.

I fall back against the couch and cover my face with my hands. I could come clean and just tell him. Then what?

Admit that I was scared. Admit that I wasn't ready to say goodbye. That I wanted to keep seeing him under the pretense of fixing Frank-E.

No. He doesn't need to know any of that. I'll ask to get together. Socially. Not to fix Frank-E. Then I'll slip the coupler into his workshop while we're there. If he wants to see me socially.

It's forgivable. It's only a little dishonest. He'd never know the underhanded lengths I'd gone to see him again.

I should shower before I ping him, but I don't want to wash his smell off me. Not yet.

"Vidping Anders, please," I call out to the room.

The comms pings, and the view screen opens in front of me. Anders's smiling face peers at me from the holoscreen. His hair is wet, and the lights in the room dim. Was he getting ready for bed?

"This is a nice surprise." His smile is wide.

I don't even say "'lo" before I hold up the ring to show him. "I have the coupler."

Ugh. So much for my stealth plan. *Don't confess. Don't confess.* "I found it." The words burst out of my mouth.

"That's great." His smile grows wider, and his eyes crinkle at me. He knows I took it. He must.

This is why I don't lie. I'm terrible at it.

"Now I can finish fixing Frank-E," he says.

"Sure. Maybe next week."

"Oh." His smile dims.

"I was wondering," I continue before I lose my nerve. "Spring Fest is this weekend. We could celebrate together. Then deal with bot stuff later. It's waited this long. What's another week?"

His smile returns, radiating at three times the lumens. "I would love to." An impish grin transforms his face from happy to mischievous. "I have a condition though."

A condition? The ultimatum stabs me in the chest.

"What?" I ask, caution coloring my voice.

"I have a present for you. I was going to give it to you after we fixed Frank-E. But I'd like you to wear it this weekend."

"Oh" is all I can think to say. *A present? For me?* My own smile spreads so wide my cheeks start to hurt.

He holds up a white box wrapped with a green ribbon. "I can get it couriered over before Friday."

"Tonight?"

He laughs. "Tonight then."

"Can you open it now so I can see it?"

He laughs. "No. You'll have to wait until you get it."

An hour later, the courier arrives with my gift, and as I promised before ending our call earlier, I vidping him before opening the box.

With him watching, I unlace the bow and open the box. Folded inside is an emerald-green garment made of the softest silkweave fibers. Maneuvering it to make sense of what it is, I find the shoulders and hold it up. It's a shrug. Essentially, the sleeves and upper torso of a cardigan.

"I love it," I say. "Of course I'll wear it."

13

Spring Fest

Gwen

I answer the door wearing a strapless white dress that hugs my generous curves from the top of my breasts to mid-thigh. My high-heeled spikes match the green of the shrug covering my shoulders and arms. My hair is loose and wavy, spilling over my shoulders. I toss it back, giving him a view of the shrug.

My move has the desired effect, and his jaw drops. For a Dominant with the ability to master another's body, he loses his composure with little effort on my part. As much as I fantasize about giving up control to this man, I like having this bit of power.

He tells me he has plans for me. I am open to anything he wants to show me. My only hope is that by the end of the night all I'm wearing is this shrug and these heels.

"Can you walk in those shoes?" he asks, taking my hands without hesitation. Heat blossoms from my heart and radiates over my skin. I thrill at his confident touch, no longer tentative and careful with me. He steps back to admire me, and his obvious appreciation sends a jolt to my lower belly.

"Barely, but it's worth the look on your face."

His brow furrows with worry, and I laugh. "I'm joking. These shoes are made for dancing."

Sharing laughter and touches, an easy familiarity, comes naturally with Anders. I forgot how much I like it. Need it. With Anders, I'm hungry for it.

We stroll through the market gallery, where open-air cafés and restaurants thrum with the bustle of the night. Many restaurants are holding Spring Fest parties, and the air is festive with sultry, rhythmic music flowing out of businesses and twinkling lights over the entire promenade.

We're going to the Spring Fest party at a Brazilian-Japanese restaurant in the heart of the international market. The energy in the restaurant is vibrant and loud, but from where we're seated in a corner booth with no view of the band and a partial view of the dance floor, we don't notice.

"I'm happy you wore the shrug," he says. It frames my breasts before sweeping under my arms. The contemplative look he gives me as his gaze rakes over my body raises gooseflesh on my skin.

"I love it. I would've worn it even if it wasn't a condition."

"I have to admit, I'm dying to see it on you with lingerie."

"Oh, no," I say, my tone apologetic. "That might be a problem."

"Why?"

Looking down at my dress, I sidle against him on the padded bench. "I'm not wearing anything under this dress."

His brown eyes grow black in the candlelight, and his hand drops to my thigh. I smile sweetly. He returns my smile with a coy smirk and slides his hands between my thighs, unconcerned about anyone nearby. I spread my legs for him, and he slides his hand up, pushing my skirt aside to stroke my pussy.

"So wet. The things I'm going to do to this pussy later."

I release a decadent sigh and lean against him to whisper, "Yes, please."

"You are a naughty girl, aren't you?"

My memory flashes on my theft of the coupling ring.

"I am," I say. I had planned to tell him another time. In the future. But the guilt of the lie has been wearing on me. "I have something to confess."

"Okay." Concern steals some of the wrinkles around his eyes.

"I took the coupler out of your bag." I rush with my confession, unable to keep the secret any longer.

His smile turns crooked. "Why?"

"I was worried that once you fixed Frank-E, we wouldn't have occasion to meet again. It was irrational, but it happened so fast, I didn't reason it out at the time."

"You really are a naughty girl, aren't you?" His tone becomes playful, and it's clear he's not concerned about the deception. "Do you know what happens to bad girls?"

"No." The word is a gasp as the syrupy croon of his voice licks at all my needy parts. "What happens to bad girls?"

"They get punished."

The warmth that spreads between my legs is liquid at his words. If I'm going to be naughty, I might as well be naughty. I lean against him and ask, "Do they get spanked?"

His jaw drops open for the second time this evening. Then his tongue swipes out to wet his lips. He nods.

"At the club?"

His smile is pure mischief. "Eventually."

Anders

Dinner is delicious, the conversation fun, and before long the rhythm of the music calls us to the dance floor. We join the crush of people jumping, swaying, and grinding to the sultry pounding of Afro-Latin sonica. Pressed together, amidst the dynamic frenzy of pure kinetic energy, we learn each other's bodies. Its electrifying force sweeps us into the open gallery to blend with the revelers of all the parties throughout the market in a carnival-style fervor.

I never let her go, leading her, spinning her, and pressing her to me at every opportunity. She grips, caresses, and grinds on me at all the right moments. We could've danced all night, but when she takes my hand and maneuvers us out of the crowd, I follow blindly, hypnotized by her sway.

Flush with the need to take the dancing home, I let her lead me out of the market gallery.

14

The Sum of Parts

Gwen

Anders opens a bottle of wine. He has no plan, but I do. He's waiting for me. Has been all this time. It's up to me to hand over control.

I stand in the middle of the sitting area, in full view of Anders, and unfasten my dress.

He notices and watches me, working the bottle in his hands distractedly.

I slip the dress down slowly, revealing my full breasts, my rounded stomach and hips, and my generous thighs. I step out of the dress and drape it over a nearby chair.

My core tightens with awareness under his watchful gaze.

I turn sideways, wearing only emerald-green heels and the silky green shrug, my shoulders rolled back so the panels frame my breasts. Then I kneel on the ground in the perfect submissive posture, buttocks on heels, hands on knees, and eyes cast downward. I wish I could see his face.

The taut energy in the air resonates through me and ripples over my skin.

When he comes to stand in front of me, he's barefoot. He's kicked off his shoes. This detail sends another chill through my body.

He cups my chin and tilts my face to meet his gaze. His smile is wicked and wanting, and I melt. I'm sure my now-throbbing pussy is slick for him.

"Aren't you a pretty present?"

"For you, sir," I say, unable to keep the smile off my face when his lips part, and his throat bobs.

"Tonight you're my toy," he says as he runs his thumb over my bottom lip. "Would you like that?"

"Yes, sir," I answer, wanting nothing more.

He walks in a circle around me.

When he's standing before me again, he says, "You like being a bad girl?"

"I fantasize about being a bad girl."

"You think about being punished? About spankings?"

"Yes, sir."

He holds out his hand, and when I take it, he pulls me to my feet and leads me to the couch. Sitting in the center, he pulls me down to lie across his lap. My bottom is propped up over his thighs while my upper body relaxes on the cushions to his side, and my legs rest on the other side of him. Goose pimples break out over my body as he rests a hand on my lower back and slides it down over my ass. His fingers brush over the backs of my thighs, and he spreads my legs as wide as he can on the cushion.

"Such a pretty ass."

He runs a finger over one ass cheek, barely an eyelash's distance from my slit. He traces a delicate line along my crack to my tailbone and down along the other side to the back of my thigh.

I arch my back and wiggle my butt in response to his lazy strokes so close to my needy pussy.

Anders *tsks*. "That's a bad girl."

Anders

I plant an open-handed smack across both ass cheeks, and she gasps.

A rosy hue flares on her ass. I plant another smack on one cheek. She rocks her hips, and I land two more spankings on either side of her ass in quick succession.

"Keep still, baby," I say.

I return to tracing lines along her cleft and outside her folds. Gwen's body is flushed with need, and looking down at the pink hue of her ass makes my cock harder, if that's even possible.

She wiggles her bottom for me, and I reward her by landing another series of light blows on each ass cheek in turn. She moans in response, and I'm tempted to kneel behind her and bite her juicy pink flesh.

She pants as she writhes, trying to grind into my lap, her dewy wetness coating the insides of her thighs. It's all I can do to keep from falling to my knees and making out with her pussy.

I slap the sweet spot where her thighs meet the globes of her ass, going back and forth in a series of rhythmic blows.

Gwen

My body tingles. The heat from his well-placed spanks radiates to my pussy. He caresses my enflamed ass, his rough hands abrading my tender skin. My mind tumbles as I struggle to reconcile the contradicting sensations.

He holds his hand still across my bottom, and I prepare myself for another round of blows. I inhale and hold my breath in anticipation. The intimacy. The closeness. My pounding heart. His hot hand. I'm slick with the thrill of the anticipated sting.

I let out a long, steady exhale as he strikes the sweet spot he's been favoring.

Heat radiates up from my throbbing depths and through my body. My eyes are closed, and I feel with my whole body. The cool air against my heated skin, the sound of his breath, the pounding of my heart throbbing all over me. I spread my legs, almost as if trying to get relief.

With three rapid snaps, Anders slaps my pussy lips. Then he lands three percussive blows directly across both cheeks. He peppers the insides of my thighs, twice on each side, before returning to my pussy. I rock against each of his blows as he follows this pattern, lulling me with the heated sensations. His blows aren't too hard, but they're precise, and they sting.

I exist only in the space that is my sex. I barely hear Anders murmuring indecipherable words of approval, but his tone is soothing, nonetheless.

Anders

Pleased with how she likes to play, I stroke one cheek. "Good tigers get rewarded," I say. "Stand up."

She obeys as she rises to her feet in front of me. I stand and tilt her face to mine.

"Tell me how your pussy feels," I command, wanting to know everything about how she feels.

"It's aching, sir." Her face is dazed and her body is relaxed, but her eyes are fixed on mine, ready for whatever comes next.

"Shall I take a look?"

"Yes, sir, please."

She started calling me "sir" on her own. It sends a shiver down my spine and makes my cock harder every time she says it.

I take her hand and lead her to stand beside the sofa. I turn her to face the cushions wide enough to support her body, and stand behind her. I reach around to cup her full breasts and toy with her nipples. I tug at them roughly and pinch them. With my body pressed to her back, I sense each of her responses. Her gasps, the rolling of her hips, and the goose pimples that cover her skin are my reward for playing these games. When I press my hard cock against her back, her breathing grows labored, and she whimpers against the cushions.

After I'm satisfied that my little tortures have driven her arousal to a new level, I release her breasts and push her forward so she's bent over the backrest of the couch, her upper body stretched along its length. I press my weight against her back as I take her hands and raise them over her head. She lets out another gasp, and my heart races when I feel her shudder beneath me.

"Don't let go," I whisper in her ear.

I want to take my time getting to know her kinks. I am not in a hurry to bind her. But her response to being ordered not to move is so lovely, I know she'll enjoy being tied up. Later. We have time to learn each other.

I lift myself and move to kneel behind her. She waits patiently for me, and I wait a few heartbeats before touching her again. When I finally do, I grip her ass cheeks with both hands and spread her lips with my thumbs to expose her cunt to me completely.

I can tell she's holding her breath. When I lick her, her breath gushes out audibly, and I get to work. I inhale deeply and lap at her entrance, drinking in her taste and her scent.

"Such a delicious pussy," I tell her before I swirl my tongue inside her, drawing out more of her moisture.

Gwen

He licks me, running his tongue over my clit, then returning to dip into my cunt. My awareness narrows. There is nothing but his hands and mouth on my flesh.

"I like it when you call me 'sir.'" His voice is measured and controlled, and I'm lost in its soothing tenor.

He shifts his position to stand behind me. I can only moan in response.

"If you want me to stop, you can say 'red,' okay?"

"Yes, sir."

At my words he begins fucking me with his fingers. He pumps a few times and stops again, leaving me whimpering.

"Do you know how delicious you taste?"

"Yes," I say, remembering the taste of my cum on his mouth. I throb at the memory.

He strokes my ass with one hand, and I feel something thick at my entrance. His cock.

"Hmm. Such a dirty tiger. You like the taste of your cunt, don't you?"

"Yes," I whisper against the couch cushion just loud enough for him to hear.

I let out a low moan as he slides in an inch and pulls out. He's slow and gentle, filling me deeper with each thrust. And with a few slow pumps, he's all the way inside me, his hips pressing against my ass. I arch against him, my fingers gripping the cushions over my head. I dare not release my grip, eager to see what he's planning.

"Yes," I whisper against the couch cushion just loud enough for him to hear.

He fucks me, sliding in and out in long thrusts that stroke my inner walls sumptuously. He pulls out. Again, the shock of his absence leaves me cold, yet simultaneously hot with wanting.

"Stand up, Sexy."

I do as he says, slightly disoriented, and he leads me to the couch. He sits down. His cock, slick with my juices, is an angry purple.

"Come here and taste yourself."

I gasp at the filthiness of his order, but my body responds with a flood of tingling need from my scalp to my toes. He tugs at my hand, and eager to comply, I kneel on the cushions next to him. He pushes my hair off to one side so he can watch, and on hands and knees, I lower my face to his cock.

"That's it, Tiger, lick yourself off me like the most delicious ice cream in the world. I want you to taste what I taste."

Hungry for him, I lick his cock in long strokes, cleaning my salty, sweet musk off him. I grip his cock at the base and moan as I lap at him. He holds my hair away from my face with one hand, the other stroking my back.

After I lick him clean, I take his cock in my mouth as deep as I can, resuming where he left off earlier.

His hand reaches over my ass and then strokes my pussy from behind. He drives his fingers inside, and when he resumes fucking me, I take the entire length of him into my mouth, swallowing around his cock as I work to take him deeper.

"Fuck," he says on a guttural moan, and then he's shifting position.

He drops to his side, and he lifts me, forcing me to let go of his cock, and before I realize his intention, he's flat on his back underneath me. In a few smooth and strategic moves, I'm straddling his face.

"So much better," he murmurs as he licks my pussy with a zeal that leaves me breathless.

He drives my pace as I take his cock in my mouth again. His fingers fuck me, and his tongue lavishes my clit as I wrap my hands around his ass and encourage him to thrust up into my mouth. Once he's tilting his hips up rhythmically, I reach to cup his balls with one hand.

The sloppy, wet sounds of lapping and sucking fill the space around us. His movements are jerky, but so are mine. Our fucking is hard and desperate with tongues and lips and throats and hands. I lose myself in the sensation of being fucked at both ends.

His fingers get thicker as he slides another finger inside me, and then he stops suddenly to adjust. But I don't stop, driven to make him cum down my throat.

Then I feel a finger press against my ass, slick with my own wetness, as his other fingers return to my pussy. He plunges into my ass, and I drop onto his cock to his base. I choke and swallow, loving the feel of being fucked everywhere. The tightening in my belly as my body strives for its release has me wound so tight I could shatter.

His hips continue thrusting into my mouth. My hunger at this moment is so deep and urgent. I spread my legs wider, pressing against him, as I grunt around his cock.

Fuck me, fuck me, fuck me, I chant in my head until the damn breaks, and I'm cumming all over his face.

My pussy and ass clench around him, the noises coming out of me primal. I bob up and down on him trying to match the pace of his increasing thrusts as I ride out my orgasm on his hands.

"I'm cumming," he warns, and though I'm ready when he spurts down my throat, I choke a little, startled by the sudden jets. I manage to swallow most of it down.

Gripping my ass cheeks hard with both hands, he laps at my pussy as I lick at him, desperate to catch every drop and clean him up.

As the waves of pleasure subside, I slump onto him, nuzzling his semi-hard dick.

After we've caught our breath, he repositions us, so I'm draped over him, and we're laying face to face, sticky and sated.

"You are fucking amazing," he says into my hair.

"Mmm," I agree. "We are amazing."

He kisses the top of my head, and I feel him smiling against my scalp. "We are."

There's a shower in our near future. And fucking. So much fucking. For now, we rest.

Later in bed, my eyes closed, I say sleepily, "I've been thinking that maybe I should retire Frank-E."

Anders props himself up on an elbow at my side. "Really? Why?"

"I think you made a good point about moving on and trying new things, or in this case, newer models."

"I hope I didn't sour you on your vintage bot. He has his charms." He traces the lines of my collar bones, and I can feel him watching me.

"No. I think it's just a good idea to let past things go."

"So, you're going to look for something new?"

"I thought you could help me find some flashy multi-purpose domestic bot."

"I can absolutely do that," he says, nuzzling my ear.

"In the meantime, maybe you could help me with my domestic needs," I say, teasing.

"Well, I'm qualified to cook, make household repairs, and provide mind-blowing orgasms on demand, so I'm definitely qualified to fulfill any needs a bot may not."

"Cleaning?"

"Simon can do that," he says with a laugh before cupping my face with his wandering hand.

He presses his lips to mine in a gentle kiss and leisurely makes love to my mouth with a tenderness that has me sighing into him. I revel in his warm flesh, breathy chuckles, and just a hint of predictability.

Acknowledgements

Thank you to Lindsey Hinkel, the best editor an author can ever hope to be fated to work with. My wonderful beta readers, Sigh and Taylor Bullet. I'm grateful every day to be able to work with this kind, fun, and talented group of creatives.

About the Author

Megan Landon is an Austin-based writer of erotic fantasy and sci-fi romance. Her stories are inspired by nature, science, language, her Columbian and Dutch roots, her linguistic training, and magic. She writes intelligent heroines, supportive heroes, dark romance, and slightly off-center worlds. As a badass mother, daughter, wife, sister, scholar, and traveler who lives in the reality of the human condition, Meg admits losing oneself in fiction is the sport of literature. Megan Landon has a PhD in linguistics. Her erotic flash fiction has appeared in Bust Magazine, and she is a regular collaborator with the Erotica Consortium.

To receive updates about upcoming releases and access art and related media, sign up for Megan's newsletter at www.meganlandon.com.